A DREAM UNFOLDS

NOELA FOX

A
DREAM
UNFOLDS

THE STORY OF NANO NAGLE

the columba press

First published in 2016 by

the columba press

55A Spruce Avenue, Stillorgan Industrial Park,
Blackrock, Co. Dublin

Cover design by Helene Pertl | The Columba Press

Origination by The Columba Press
Printed by ScandBook AB, Sweden

ISBN 978 1 78218 236 8

EXPLANATION OF TERMS

Apostasy: The abandonment of a religious or political belief or principle. In 1786 Bishop Butler, on the death of his nephew, the eleventh Lord Dunboyne, left the priesthood and his diocese, to assume the title of the twelfth Lord Dunboyne and to marry.

Jansenism: Jansenism is a Catholic theological movement which began in 1638, primarily in France. It emphasised original sin, the sinfulness of the world and the human person and claimed that salvation was reserved for a few. The Church has declared it heretical on many occasions, such as 1654, 1665 and 1705.

Oath of Abjuration: The oath required that a person renounce the Pope's supremacy and authority over the Catholic Church and deny transubstantiation and the existence of purgatory. Passed in 1643 and reissued in 1656, its penalties were the confiscation of two thirds of one's goods, and the deprivation of almost all civil rights. The oath was imposed on all teachers, lawyers, clergy of the Established Church and all state office holders.

CHAPTER ONE

'Ite, missa est.' The tall young man standing behind the rock still had his hands raised. And then it happened: three sharp bird calls. To the untutored ear it sounded like the call of the wood pigeon, which frequented the area in spring and early summer. To the listeners gathered around the young man it presaged something sinister and threatening. It was a sound they had been dreading. Quickly the young man screwed the top to the bottom of the vessel he had been using and placed it on the rock table, before removing his outer garment, which he folded into a blanket. He then stepped away to join the men, who were knotted together, now smoking and talking about crops and cattle. A couple of them took rods and sat by the quickly flowing Blackwater River, dangling them near the bush branches overhanging the water. The women came forward and placed goblets, bottles of wine, beer, apple cider, water, bread and pats of butter around the wine and bread already there. They sent the wide-eyed children to play amidst the wild flowers that grew in the fields bordering the river. Ann Nagle, sitting on the blanket and holding baby Catherine in her arms, whispered to the eldest, 'Remember, Nano, what I have told you – and no Joseph, you cannot go with Nano.' Observing signs of an impending temper tantrum from Joseph, Ann hastily relented. After all, there was little time for discipline.

'Yes, Mama. Don't worry,' replied her eldest child, who enthusiastically ordered her brother David and her cousin Margaret to follow her. She took three-year-old Joseph gently with her right hand, and little frail five-year-old Ann with her other. The estate children automatically followed her. David, seeing his sister Mary wandering along by herself, ran back, took the seven-year-old by the hand and urgently tugged her along.

When the scarlet-clad soldiers crept among the trees and bushes lining the river, they saw an estate gathered for a leisurely morning – an unusual sight, but as their captain had warned them, they would see many unexpected events on this march. They gazed intently at the scene before them. In one area the women, some with babies or toddlers at their feet, were seated on logs or blankets, weaving from reeds those strange shapes with which they had become familiar on their marches across Ireland. In another, the men were smoking their pipes and chatting – no doubt complaining about crops or herds, the soldiers sourly thought. Nearby a few men, sitting on branches washed up by the river, were fishing silently. Children of all shapes and sizes, led by a girl of about nine or ten, scampered among the spring flowers, shouting and laughing.

The Captain signalled his men to stop, stay hidden, and to hold their weapons in readiness. Leaving his lieutenant with them, he strode purposely towards the men fishing. Before he could reach them, however, he was besieged by the children, who, led by the oldest girl, had streamed towards him. Bright-eyed and intelligent looking, although rather small, she stood in front of him. Thank God they're clean, he thought, not like the ragged objects they had previously seen.

'Good morning, sir,' she smiled. Startled, Captain Webb barked, 'Good morning.' Then, remembering his purpose, and thinking information is easily obtained from children, he smiled, bent down towards the girl and, in a softer tone, said to her, 'What is your name, young miss?'

'Nano, sir.' Waving her hand in one direction she finished, 'Those are my brothers and sisters, my cousin Margaret – she came from Monphin – and over there are my friends Willy, Tommy and Bridie.'

'I see!' the Captain said, nodding and smiling at all of them, 'And what are you all doing here today?'

'We're having a day off,' answered Willie and Tommy together.

'Ah! Do you have any new people here?'

The children stopped, opened wide their eyes, and shook their heads.

Nano had time for a quick thought. 'Only mother's cousin, and he brought cousin Margaret, but she's been here before,' she replied.

'That must be very nice.'

They all nodded solemnly.

'Are they staying long?'

The children all looked at Nano. 'We don't know,' she replied.

'What does your mother's cousin do?' Captain Webb queried.

A silence was broken by David, who said, 'He's good at playing games and telling stories.'

'He's a mairchin,' broke in the previously silent Bridie.

'She means a merchant,' explained Nano, continuing, 'He deals in seeds so that people can plant good ones.'

'No he doesn't!' interjected David. 'I heard him say he's interested in spirits.'

'Don't be silly, David,' said Nano angrily.

Thinking an argument was about to erupt, the Captain left quickly, making his way towards the men, who had surreptitiously and anxiously observed the Captain with the children. They observed his approach warily and silently. Had he heard anything of interest? That was the question in each man's mind. Hiding their resentment and anxiety, they grunted in reply to his greeting, not moving their pipes from their mouths, with the exception of the tall, dark-haired, well-dressed young man with the startling blue eyes. Moving his cap with one hand and his pipe with the other, he smilingly introduced himself. 'Good morning, Captain. I'm Miles Butler. Welcome.'

The Captain stared at the urbane young man. Where had he seen him before? Was he his quarry?

Ignoring the pleasantries, Captain Webb demanded: 'I came to see Garrett Nagle.'

'He's in the middle of the sea,' a little voice behind him said. The Captain turned sharply to see that some of the children had followed him. It was David who had spoken.

'He's a mairchin,' explained little Bridie.

Nano rolled her eyes. 'He might be on a boat, or in Dublin or in Cork. We haven't heard. Mother's cousin came to help us while he is away,' she said.

Her dark eyes bored into David's, willing him not to mention France.

David, about to open his mouth, closed his lips firmly and cast down his eyes.

'Why are all those soldiers playing hide and seek in the trees?' interjected Willie – 'of the sharp eyes', as he was later known.

Before the secretly furious Captain could reply, Miles, silently amused, invited the Captain and his lieutenant to dine with them. Exasperated, but not defeated, the Captain refused. He explained that they must be on their way to camp for the night. Returning to the rest of the regiment, he ordered them to march on towards the village on the other side of the river. As they left, he confided in his lieutenant that they would not march far, but would camp out of sight, just beyond the village.

'We'll keep an eye on our men. They're a rough lot; not here to honour the King, but for the food and clothing they are issued, and the bounty they are always planning to collect. I'm suspicious about these people we've just seen,' he said. 'I'll tell you tonight what I have heard of them.'

After a pause he muttered, 'I'm sure I've seen that young fellow somewhere. He's far too suave. Well educated, too.' Turning towards the Lieutenant he continued, 'You can change the colour of your hair, change many things, but you can't change your profile. Remember that, Lieutenant; that's what I'm doing now.'

Later that night, when the servants had retired and the children were in bed, Ann Nagle, her beautiful honey-coloured hair burnished by the candlelight, began her weekly letter to her husband.

My dearest Garrett,

How I long for your return. But enough of this. You will be pleased to hear that 'Black Dillon' [this was to distinguish him from 'Red Dillon', his cousin who looked after the hens] finished harvesting the apples after your departure and, as you forecast, it was a wonderful crop. For weeks, Nellie and her helpers have been baking and bottling apples. I need not do it but I did lend a hand now and then. I love the smell of our fresh apples. Ciaran and the boys are busy with field cultivation. I hope that on your return, my darling, you will be pleased with our efforts. When not working on the crops, Ciaran goes fishing for trout, and seems to have caught quite a few lately. As you know, the older children love their fish.

You will be relieved to know that our visitors arrived safely. When Mr Coppinger told us that he had brought Mr Miles Butler on one of his ships, I wondered if he would ever get here. I prepared the children well for his visit, especially Nano and David as they usually answer for the little ones, and the estate children. Nano tends to boss them around a little, but they do follow her as though she were the Pied Piper. I know darling that she is the apple of your eye, and you assure me she will be a saint one day, but sometimes she can be trying.

Since Mr Butler has arrived, we have had Sundays off, and Mr Butler is our entertainer. It has been a time of great joy for us all. I think our children, and many of the people who come, have increased their knowledge of what we value most. Sometimes, I must admit, I am pleased our Nano is such a wanderer. She talks to everyone, knows everyone and wins everyone's confidence. She came in the other day with little Willie O'Neill, whispering to me that she had heard that a Captain Bell was in the area. You remember he informed the authorities that Mr O'Shea was a priest travelling around County Kildare, saying Masses and 'upholding the Papist beliefs'? Mr O'Shea, of course, was captured, chained, imprisoned and finally transported to the American Colonies as a slave. Little Willie, who never misses anything, described a man he had seen riding around the roads near our lands, and said he had overheard his father say he thought it was Captain Bell. I heard that this Captain Bell is a cousin of Captain James O'Dell, who has been very enthusiastic in apprehending Catholic schoolteachers.

Before our get together this morning I spent extra time with the children preparing them, and I am so pleased I did. Captain Bell visited us today when we were on our outing. Thanks to Nano and little Willie, the visit was not entirely unexpected. You would have been proud of the children. Nano and David even resisted arguing, although they came perilously close. Captain Bell seems to be a charming man, but his troops are real ruffians. It is easy to imagine the atrocities attributed to such men – burning of dwellings, raping, butchering and so on. Oh! I nearly forgot to tell you that Ciaran has almost perfected his bird calls.

You will be pleased to hear that all the children are well. David works well at his lessons; Nano's interests lie else-where, but she is very good with the younger children, particularly Ann and Joseph, on whom she dotes. If we are not careful she will lead Joseph on her wild ways.

We are all longing for your safe return within the month. How I long for it.

Your ever loving,

Ann

Dear Papa,

I asked Mama if I could write to you. I do miss you, Papa. My spelling is not too good, but if you know what I am saying I don't think it matters much, do you? David is very good at it, but he can't run, jump or ride as well as I can. The little ones are all very good and happy and baby Catherine has a beautiful smile.

Mama's cousin, Mr Butler, has been staying with us. He is very nice and knows lots of things – but not as much as you. He brought our cousin Margaret too, so we play lots of games down by the river while Ciaran fishes.

Papa, you should have seen the lovely butterflies in the holly bushes after you went away. I'd like to be a butterfly so that I could fly through the sky to where you are.

Papa come home soon,

Your loving daughter,

Nano

Dear Papa,

We had great fun today down near the river. We saw soldiers in red coats. They hid in the bushes and then went away. Mr O'Halloran said that my writing and arithmetic are very good, so I can start learning some Latin. Willie's dad is teaching me about birds and some bird whistles. He is very good. When he whistles you would really believe that he is a bird.

    Come home soon, Papa, I miss you,

    Your son,

    David

Across the river and in their tent, safe from prying eyes, Captain Bell confided in Lieutenant Waters his concerns about the Nagle family. 'They are Papists, as you already know. Garrett is the infamous Joseph Nagle's brother. My brother, William, trained with Joseph as a lawyer at Lincoln's Inn, but because he is a Papist, Joseph is not able to practise by law. However, he is so canny he continues to assist his fellow Papists to avoid the sanctions of the law. He knows all the loopholes. Moreover, Garrett's wife, Ann, is related to some of the most powerful and influential families in the kingdom. Some of the Nagle family have converted to the Established Church, so that they can retain their properties; some also fled to France, but not this branch of Annakissey Nagles. There have been several attempts to confiscate their lands without much success.'

'So what happened?' asked the Lieutenant.

'There's a case going on at the present time with George Foote, who is claiming Nagle lands at Blackrock, but I doubt that he will get it. It will probably go on for years, if I know Joseph Nagle.'

'Where is Joseph Nagle?'

'He lives in Cork. The authorities keep a close eye on him.'

'I thought Garrett Nagle owned and resided at Ballygriffin. Didn't he inherit what was left of the land after the earlier confiscations? He isn't there now, so where is he?' the Lieutenant queried.

'That indeed is the question,' answered the Captain. 'On losing their lands through the Penal Laws, many of these landed gentry, including the Nagles, invested in shipping and trade, which makes it very difficult to trace their whereabouts, or what they do. I would not mind betting that smuggling goes on – even smuggling in popish priests.'

'I thought they were forbidden to exercise their ministry if not registered to do so, under the restrictions of the law, and that they had to take the Oath of Abjuration?' interjected Lieutenant Waters.

'That's true,' agreed Captain Bell. 'Although we keep trying to plug all the loopholes with further laws, many of the Papists somehow devise means to evade the consequences. I've heard rumours that Garrett Nagle is the Pretender's agent in Flanders. He is certainly absent frequently from Ireland. The problem is that the majority of the Papists would rather die than betray one another. Even many non-Papists defy the law, and its dire punishments, by hiding them or information about them.'

'What are we going to do now?' asked Lieutenant Waters.

'I don't think we will find either the teacher, or the priest, whom I'm sure that young man is, so in the morning we return to the Curragh, where we camp. From there, I will send on one of the sergeants and two men, to obtain further orders from Dublin.'

By the time the sun rose the next morning, both Mr O'Halloran and Miles Butler had disappeared. A little after sunrise, when Captain Bell and a sergeant rode through the village and along the Blackwater River, questioning any early risers about O'Halloran or Miles Butler, they were met by blank stares, and little information – just as the Captain had predicted. At her house, Ann Nagle informed them that Miles had departed early, on receiving news of an ailing uncle. As for Mr O'Halloran, he was a wanderer who drifted here and there, so perhaps they would meet up with him on the road somewhere. 'Would you like to breakfast with us, Captain?' she politely asked. The Captain, refused as politely, saying they must be on their way. As he and his sergeant rode away, curious and relieved eyes watched them ride towards the east from the barns and hedges.

CHAPTER TWO

'Papa! Papa!' screamed five little voices. The tall, dark-haired, broad-shouldered man who alighted from the carriage smiled, and opened wide his arms to embrace his children. Over their heads his dark, dancing eyes met those of Ann, holding baby Catherine in her arms. The setting sun caught the golden heads of both mother and child, seeming to encase them in halos. Disengaging himself from his children, Garrett Nagle hugged both mother and child. As the horse and carriage were taken to the stables, the family moved into the house, where the servants had prepared what looked like a feast to the famished traveller.

Although the children were bursting with questions, they were ushered away by Mollie and Johanna, the two maids in whose care they were placed. Garrett and Ann were left alone in the long, candlelit dining room. As they ate their evening meal, the first they had had together in three months, Garrett told of his visit to France, where he had spent some time with his cousins in Cambrai.

They are all well, although Cousin Elizabeth says she still misses many of her friends in Dublin. That reminds me, we must visit the Goulds in Cork. We have not seen them for some time.' Upon further questioning from Ann, Garrett told of the successful unloading from one of his ships of canvas, linen and serge in Calais and in Portugal, and of how they had evaded discovery by the British. 'But, of course, we did deliver barrels of salt beef and pork to London, as we are required to do,' he smiled. 'There they will be used by the English navy, which is struggling to maintain its superiority in the growing Empire. Fortunately, so far we have been able to expand our business, in spite of the laws which curtail our trade. Now, tell me about yourself, the children and all at Ballygriffin. I spend most of my time away thinking about you all.'

Ann's smile lit up her face as she explained their daily life, the progress of the farm, the dedicated work of the servants and farm workers, and the children's doings. Due to hard work and the favourable weather, the farm had yielded a profit. Brother Joseph had come across from Cork City several times to dine with them. 'I think he really comes to see the children,' Ann said. 'You know how much he loves them, and they him. He checks on their progress, encourages the older ones, and plays with the little ones. They become so excited when he arrives – although not as excited as they were to see you, Garrett.' At this Garrett beamed, and nodded. He then sighed, and after a pause, quietly said, 'You know, Ann, we will soon have to make arrangements to send the children away to school. Nano, of course, will go first. I know that you, the children and all the estate people will really miss her.'

There were a few moments of silence before Ann, in a small voice, replied, 'Yes, it has been on my mind for some time, Garrett. You know how she will react to that news, although I have been trying to prepare her.'

Another long silence followed. Ann continued, 'Often I have sat in this room with the children and talked to them about the pictures we have on the wall.' She glanced up at the painting of her great grandmother, Lady Thurles, as she continued, 'What a great woman she was, and how well educated. Nano is very like her with her high spirits, and the same engaging personality. Nano has never signalled any interest in this history. Come to think of it, the only one who has been interested is little Joseph, who marches around the room pretending to be a soldier, like your father, David. How wrong it is that we cannot educate our children in Ireland, just because we are Catholics.'

Garrett frowned and, shaking his head, replied, 'At least we can get our children to France on one of our ships, under the pretence of visiting relatives, and so we won't lose our lands. On my next visit, would you allow me to visit the Benedictine Nuns to organise Nano and the other girls' education, Ann? Or perhaps I can do it through Uncle Richard in France. I could request my uncles, James and Richard, to keep an eye on them, and care for them during holidays. I could also ask Uncle James's advice on the boys' education, because he would have had experience with his son, Garrett, and David will soon follow Nano to school.'

Ann sighed, and looked up at the family portraits, seeking unheard advice from previous generations, before agreeing.

In the coming months, Ann was preoccupied with worries and thoughts of the children: How will they cope with being away from their beloved Ballygriffin and all their friends? How will Nano manage the challenges to her freedom and to her dislike of book learning? She will miss her sparring with David, and the love of the little ones. What would they all do without her? Perhaps they could send Mary to join her earlier than they had planned.

Now that Mr O'Halloran had disappeared for a time, Ann continued the education of her children. They were all aware of the penalties they would suffer if they were discovered learning, especially about their faith. The servants, Mollie and Johanna, would often regale the older children with stories of families who had been driven off their lands because they taught their children. Sometimes more gruesome stories were told of travelling schoolmasters, who, when they were discovered, were hanged, or sent away as slaves. They were always quick to add that Mr O'Halloran was too smart to be caught. Nano and

David's eyes would gleam with excitement, Mary's with apprehension, and Joseph would march about shouting, 'I'm going to be a soldier and kill the English!'

'Oh! Joseph! You can't be a soldier,' Nano would laugh as she caught him. 'We aren't allowed to be soldiers, or even own a gun.'

'No, we can't,' agreed David.

'When we grow up we might be able to think of something, but no killing,' said Nano.

'Yes,' agreed David, rather doubtfully.

Garrett busily divided his time between his family, the estate manager, his shipping office in Cork, and his brother Joseph. Joseph lived in Dundanion, Blackrock, near Cork, with his faithful housekeeper, his servants and his beloved dog, a black setter with a broad grin, called Nimy. When asked by an inquisitive Nano where Nimy got his name, Uncle Joseph replied, 'He's named after our family castle Monanimy, of course.'

One quiet autumn evening, when the soft shadows were growing long, and Garrett and Ann were enjoying an evening together before a flickering fire, Garrett broke the companionable silence to confide in Ann his concerns about a portion of their Ballygriffin lands. Ann had noticed that for some days Garrett was preoccupied, but said nothing, knowing that when the time was right he would confide in her.

'Ann, remember some time back I had to lease some of our land to the Protestant Peter Graham?'

With trepidation, Ann replied, 'Yes, dear.'

'Well, I'm having problems over land again.'

Looking alarmed, Ann exclaimed, 'Oh! I hope we aren't going to lose more land! Are you thinking of going to see Joseph about it?'

'Yes, I'll travel to Cork tomorrow. I'll only be away a couple of days, Ann. Remember the last time we had a problem over the land, Joseph advised me to lease Ballymacallin to Peter Graham, so he will give me good advice again.'

Early the next morning Garrett, accompanied by Eamon, the coachman, rode south-east towards Cork City, where they arrived later that day at Dundanion. The door was opened by the portly figure of Joseph himself.

'Welcome! A thousand welcomes, Garrett!' The delighted Joseph embraced his brother, then directed Eamon to take the horse and carriage to the stables, and himself to the kitchen for a warm meal.

Later, over a meal, the brothers shared family news. Garrett waxed eloquent over his beautiful, capable Ann, of her loving care of the children and the property whenever he was absent. Joseph nodded in agreement, and eventually asked about the children. Garrett, knowing Joseph's interest was chiefly centred on his favourite, Nano, chuckled. 'Nano is as lively as ever. Her writing is quite scrawly, and she is not interested in those sampler things girls are supposed to excel at. Mind you, she could do them very well if she put her mind to them, but she can't see the use for them. She would much rather watch the men plaster the barns. Ann is always concerned she will never develop into a real lady. I tell Ann she has the qualities that really matter in our world – she's strong-willed, loyal, lively, has a loving heart, is practical, makes friends easily – and most certainly won't suffer from the vapours.' Joseph beamed, while Garrett expounded on the virtues of his other children. The next morning, the brothers conferred over the serious matters of how to retain as much as possible of their land, and their shipping business, under the restrictions of the Penal Laws. Joseph advised Garrett to sell the parcel of land he had previously leased to Peter Graham, in order to avoid further trouble. Nano's education was next discussed. Where would she go on the Continent? How would she get there without detection by the English? How could her absence from Ballygriffin be explained? It was essential that all would be accomplished in secret.

'We will need to think of the boys' education soon,' Garrett said to his brother, 'but for now we'll concentrate on Nano, as she will have to go in the near future.'

When Garrett returned to Ballygriffin, he shared with Ann the decisions made. Some weeks later, when the weak autumn sun had set and the children were in bed, Garrett broke the news that he would have to return to France as soon after Christmas as the weather permitted.

'Will you be taking Nano with you?' Ann asked softly.

'I'm afraid so, Ann.' There was a short pause before Garrett continued gently, 'I contacted the Benedictines. You know that many Nagles have been educated by them, and they are happy to have another member of the family. She won't be alone; Uncle Richard and his family will care for her, and I'm sure she will make friends with her cousins. You know how friendly and happy Nano always is. Then, of course there will be my visits, and you could come sometimes, too, Ann.'

'Yes, Garrett,' replied Ann in a tremulous voice, 'I suppose she will soon be joined by Mary, and David will be going nearby next year.'

'It's strange,' Ann continued, 'I have to correct Nano so often for her unladylike behaviour, but I don't know how I will manage without her. She is so caring with the little ones, and seems to be aware of everything which goes on around the farm. Oh, these Penal Laws! What heartbreak and sorrow they bring!'

In late December, Ann, with the other children and the servants, stood at the front door to bid farewell to Garrett and Nano. As the carriage sped down the driveway, Nano looked back through the carriage window at the tableau framed in the doorway. She saw her mother, obviously struggling with her emotions, hugging baby Catherine to herself; a loudly crying Joseph clinging to his mother's skirts on one side; and Ann quietly sobbing and hiding her face in the skirt's folds on the other side. To the side, David and Mary were holding hands and stoically endeavouring to suppress their tears. Nano watched, her face pressed to the glass, and waved until she could no longer see them, and it was then she saw the estate children, waving and shouting as they weaved in and out of the trees lining the driveway. Amongst them were Bridie, Willie and Tommy, waving and shouting, their sturdy legs pumping up and down, as they chased the carriage. Long after they had disappeared from sight, Nano kept her eyes glued to the window, hoping that somehow she would catch another glimpse of them all.

CHAPTER THREE

'Miss Nagle!' The voice seemed to come from a distance. The years had passed so quickly. Nano had been seeing in her mind the scene from long ago, when she had travelled down the drive from Ballygriffin.

Tomorrow, she thought, I'll be leaving here.

Before she could examine her feelings, the voice broke into her thoughts.

'Yes, Mother Augustine,' Nano dutifully answered.

'Mother Superior would like to see you in the second parlour, to finalise the arrangements for your departure tomorrow, when your uncle's carriage arrives, Miss Nagle.'

'Yes, thank you, Mother Augustine,' Nano once more answered as she followed the tall, graceful Mother Augustine down the long, dim corridor to the second parlour, where she was greeted by the smiling Mother Superior. Nano smiled in return, thinking no doubt Mother Superior is smiling with relief, as I certainly wasn't the most dedicated student. However, she would be very happy with Mary and Ann, both of whom work really hard. Mary is quite bright, and Ann is a darling.

Nano would have been pleasantly surprised if Mother Benedict had revealed her thoughts. As Nano sat on one of the high-backed, intricately carved oak chairs, Mother Benedict silently reflected that here was a high-spirited, intelligent, engaging young woman, who threw herself wholeheartedly into whatever she undertook; please God, she thought, it will not be the social life of Paris, or some wild scheme doomed to failure.

Nano, of course, was thinking that from tomorrow, she would be free to dance, or ride when or where she liked (preferably with that handsome Compte de Sullis), to come and go as she wished, to stay in bed, to get up— Again her thoughts were interrupted by Mother Benedict's arrangements for her departure the next morning, and her advice on how she was to behave as a daughter of the renowned Nagle family. Although Nano endeavoured to look attentive and impressed, even managing the correct responses as required, she struggled to control her excitement at the thought of tomorrow's freedom.

The following morning, Nano's great-uncle Sir Richard Nagle's carriage arrived at precisely 10 a.m. While Nano's belongings were being loaded, she said farewell to the many friends she had made, promising to visit them as soon as she had settled into her uncle's home, or, if they were returning to Ireland, to see them upon her own return. Over the years, Nano had returned infrequently to Ballygriffin, and as such had greatly enjoyed the visits from her father when he was on business to France. He always brought letters from her mother, who rarely came, informing her of the events and people she knew. Uncle Joseph wrote frequently, telling her about Nimy's activities, and then of her death. Soon Nimy was replaced by Nimytwo, whom Uncle Joseph described in affectionate words. There were hints of darker happenings, which Garrett described on his visits when Nano asked about them. Sometimes, too, the younger children wrote, and Nano had avidly read and re-read their letters. However, on this final day of her schooling Nano's thoughts were on the joys she would experience in this city, known as 'the city of elegance'.

Mary, and Ann, who had come to join Nano at school, would spend the vacations with her. David, who had arrived the year after Nano, was still at school in Ypres with Joseph, who had arrived a couple of years later. Nano saw both frequently, and was always overjoyed when they arrived and she could hear their plans for the future. David was so anxious to return to Ballygriffin. His main topic of conversation was how he would manage the properties he would someday inherit. Nano would remind him that, according to the Penal Laws, lands owned by Catholics had to be gravelled, that is divided between sons on the death of their father. That was unless one turned Protestant, in which case he could have it all, a measure devised to curtail Catholics' ownership of land. Scornfully, David would robustly declare that he would not change his religion. Joseph would quickly respond that he didn't want the land – he'd be a soldier to fight the English, or maybe he would be a lawyer like Uncle Joseph, and change the law.

Nano would hug him and laughingly retort, 'Oh! Joseph! You'll have to be a lawyer. If you are a soldier you will break Mama's heart. She'll be so worried about you.'

Joseph would nod, and smile what Nano called his secret smile.

On that morning when Nano left the school for the last time, as the carriage sped down the roads, she was unaware of the ragged groups crouched in corners, endeavouring to escape the bitter winds that pierced their tatters and to bit into their thin-framed bodies. The carriage hurtled on, through the tree-lined avenues guarding graceful homes, until it reached the iron gates enclosing the long, sheltered driveway which led to Uncle Richard's residence at Cambrai. The gates were swung open by liveried servants. The coach was driven through the gardens, past the fountain, to come to a stop at the foot of the marble steps of the front entrance. Here Nano was joyfully met by her uncle, aunt and many cousins.

The next morning Nano was awakened by Johanna, now her maid, who set by her bedside a silver tray, on which was a silver teapot and cutlery, all emblazoned with the Nagle crest. After a cheery good morning, Johanna flung back the heavy drapes that covered the windows, and Nano, struggling to open her eyes, saw on the tray a selection of pastries and jams. Johanna reminded Nano that later in the day, she, along with her cousins, James, Pierre, Elizabeth and Jane, would be visiting one of the salons. The day would be spent preparing for the visit, beginning with the hairdresser, who would arrive mid-morning. So began Nano's years of enjoying the pleasures of the fashionable city. Later, looking back on these years, Nano was to confess that she enjoyed everything so much that she began to think she could live happily nowhere else in the world.

On his visits, Garrett would bring letters from Ann and the children, together with news of the sad plight of the people, especially after the 'great frosts' of 1737 and 1741. 'Even around Ballygriffin', Garrett told them, 'people are starving because the crops and the fruit on the trees have been burnt, and the cattle are dying for lack of food.'

'So, what are the people doing?' asked Nano. Ann, who had left school and was now residing with Nano, was particularly concerned.

'Unfortunately they have to walk to the cities, particularly Cork, Dublin and Limerick. But many die on the roads,' replied their father.

'Whatever are they going to do in the city?' asked Ann.

'Sad to say, they crowd the cities, where conditions are little better. They live in freezing garrets and basements, which, especially in Cork, are damp and often flooded. You remember Cork is built on reclaimed marshlands, and there is no drainage. Some say that over a quarter of the population has died from fevers or starvation.'

'How terrible!' Nano and Ann exclaimed in unison.

'Can't they get any work?' asked the ever-practical Nano. She could think of nothing worse than being cold and hungry;

having to work from morning until night ranked a close second. But then, she thought, some people have to.

'There is very little available,' Garrett explained. 'Once we had thriving industries – wool and flax manufacturing, and we could export meat products like beef and pork. But now, on account of the Penal Laws of 1699 and those following, strict restrictions have been placed on all our manufacturing and trade, and there is little work for anyone, including farmers. Even in our shipping we are not free but by law must carry goods to the Royal Navy or the English Colonies, like the West Indies and the Americas.'

'Oh Papa!' cried Ann, her heart contracting at the thought of so much suffering. 'What happens to the little children?' Nano began to think of their own childhood, when they had scampered over the wooden stile and run down the winding road to the ruin of Monanimy castle, where they would be tutored by Mr O'Halloran, always under the watchful eye of one of the estate men, on guard against any informer. As children, they had been told of the necessity for maintaining secrecy over their schooling, but had not fully recognised the bravery and faith of their parents, their teacher and those who protected them. Only since coming to France for their education had the full implications of these Penal Laws gradually dawned on the Nagle children. One evening, when Nano and Ann were having supper with their cousins at Cambrai, Cousin Elizabeth remarked, 'Where did you learn to read so well, Ann? My father told us that Catholic children in Ireland were not allowed to be educated. Actually he said you were forbidden to come overseas for education as well.'

Ann explained how they went to the ruins of the castle, which had once belonged to the Nagle family, and how Mr O'Halloran pretended to be a wandering workman so that he could avoid capture. Nano added, 'He taught us about our religion, although Mama taught us more of that, also reading, writing and arithmetic, as well as some of our old poems and our history. He taught David some Latin, and I suppose he taught Joseph some too, but I had left by then.'

'Yes, he did,' added Ann.

'He was a very brave man,' Nano reflected. 'Now I wish I had been a better scholar. Do you remember, Ann, when we were children, and that captain and his men came to Ballygriffin, when we were at Mass down near the river? I think he was looking for Mr O'Halloran, or Mama's priest cousin, Father Miles.'

'I wonder where they are now?' mused Ann.

'I don't know. I hope they haven't been discovered, or if they were, that they had time to escape to France. I remember Mama telling me, I think it was after Elizabeth was born, that Bishops MacCarthy of Cork and O'Keefe of Limerick, when they found that an informer had disclosed them, avoided capture by fleeing to Nantes.' Nano continued, 'How brave Mama and Papa have been. If it was discovered how they educated us and harboured priests, they would lose everything. One day when, or if, I return, I'm going to thank all the estate people and all our neighbours, because if they had informed the authorities they would have been granted half our wealth. I don't think I could be as selfless.'

'Aren't you ever going home, Nano?' asked an alarmed Ann.

'Oh, yes!' Nano said, then added somewhat dismissively, 'When I'm old. I'm having such a wonderful time here. Are you coming to the ball tonight?'

'Really Nano, I don't think I can. Tomorrow we will be out most of the day at Jean Baptiste Greuze's wonderful art exhibition in the Royal Academy. Last night we were at that brilliant young musician Mozart's concert, and the night before we were at that salon – I forget the name – we go to so much.

I don't know how you keep up with all these events. However, I know you really enjoy the arguments, the discussions and sharing new ideas, especially on the place of women in our society. You always have an opinion and are not afraid to voice it. I do wish I could do that, but it all makes me so tired. What time is your hair appointment? Last time it took three hours, so you need to hurry.'

'Ann, you are a darling – always thinking of other people. Yes, I must hurry, because I also have to get dressed in that new dress I bought. Ann, you should see it. It's magnificent. It's a soft sky blue with silver brocade, and I'll wear the diamond necklace Papa gave me for my birthday.' Ann smiled proudly at her 'big' sister, whose eyes sparked in anticipation of the evening.

'I suppose you have reserved places on your dance card for that Compe de Sallis, who, I must admit, is very handsome.'

'Yes, he is handsome,' Nano agreed, then added, 'but he's a bit of a fop. I can't discuss important things with him. Have you seen the Duc de Chartres? He dances superbly, and has such wonderful manners, so I hope he asks me. I'm keeping some dances for him just in case. And then there is Maurice de Saxe, who looks so dashing in his uniform. I heard whispers that he is a commander with the Irish Brigade.'

Ann laughed. She was getting used to Nano enumerating all her dance partners. 'You have always heard all the news, Nano, even when we were children. Is he really a commander in the King's army? I've heard Joseph mention him as a great commander. Poor Papa, he was so upset when Joseph joined the Irish Brigade. I hope he remains safe. I think he can be a little rash sometimes.'

'I wasn't surprised when he joined the Irish Brigade,' said Nano. 'Do you remember he was always playing at being a soldier, and just loved the stories about Grandfather David, who was a captain and fought in the defence of Cork in 1690, against John Churchill, the Earl of Maryborough. Grandfather was lucky he didn't lose everything, or was not exiled like his poor brothers, after they were defeated. Ann! Look at the time! I'll really have to hurry.' With these words Nano summoned Johanna to begin her preparations.

Nano's evening at the ball surpassed all her expectations. Not a place on her dance card was empty. The conversations were witty and entertaining, and though she was not overly interested in the food, Nano did admire its artistic presentation. Beneath a myriad of chandeliers she waltzed, danced the minuet and the cotillion, under the watchful eye of her aunt, the chaperone for her dazzling niece, who captivated and entranced many an eye. Nano's dress, sparkling with silver thread, fell from her shoulders to swirl in silver circles about her feet. Her partners were as expensively dressed. The Duc de Chartres was amongst those most richly attired, the buttonholes of his coat sewn with diamonds.

The years have passed so quickly, mused Nano, as the carriage bumped and lurched over the worn cobblestones, as it took her home after another night of dancing. It was almost time for the sun to wanly struggle to a new day. She pulled back the window drapes, to peer at the rain misting the window. She narrowed her eyes. Surely that is not people huddled together near the church door, she thought.

'Aunt!' she exclaimed to her long-suffering aunt, who dozed in the corner.

'Aunt! What on earth are those poor, tattered people doing at this hour?'

Her aunt's eyes jerked open, and slowly focused on the scene.

'Oh! My dear, they are waiting for the church to open for Mass.'

'Mass!' Nano frowned in bewilderment. Her happy and peaceful reminiscences of the night were replaced by a disturbance she could not fathom. She hastily closed the curtains, and endeavoured to blot the image from her mind. Her aunt leant back, closed her eyes and appeared to sleep. Nano, too, closed her eyes, hoping that the image of the shivering, ill-clad figures would disappear from her sight. She had partly succeeded by the time the carriage jolted to a stop; the doors were opened by the footmen, and she, with her aunt, was helped from the coach and up the steps into the warm embrace of their home.

Unusually for her, Nano spent a restless night. Haggard faces and pleading eyes floated in and out of her dreams. The next day as she sat in her boudoir, she saw Johanna reflected in the mirror, straightening her gowns in the wardrobe. Without warning, the scene from the night before flashed into her mind. She turned.

'Johanna,' she said, 'I really don't think I need all those clothes. Are there some I haven't worn for a while?'

Johanna hid a smile at the thought of all the clothes Nano seldom wore again.

'Yes, Miss Nano,' she replied.

'Could you please sort out any I haven't worn for a time, pack them up, and send them to some poor women. Miss Ann would know some, I'm sure.'

Johanna obeyed with alacrity. Miss Nano is sometimes heedless, but has always had a kind heart, she thought.

Her conscience appeased for a time, Nano continued her preparations for the rest of the day. Sometimes accompanied by Ann, or one of her young cousins, always chaperoned by her aunt or one of her married cousins, Nano continued her visits to the salons, the galleries, the gardens, or to one of her many relations, or the families of the Irish exiles.

'Miss Nano! It's a beautiful day,' announced Johanna one morning as she drew the richly brocaded curtains of Nano's room.

The sun's warm, slanted fingers shimmered across the bed where Nano, shaking out her hair, was just getting up. At that moment, a soft knock at the door announced the arrival of Ann, already dressed and prepared for the day. Ann's face lit with her gentle smile – but before she could begin a conversation with her sister, there was another knock, and the French maid, without a word, handed a silver tray to Johanna, who with a glance at the letter there, took it to Nano.

'Oh! It's a letter from Uncle Joseph. How wonderful!'

Excitedly, Nano opened the letter with her ivory letter opener. Looking on, Ann saw Nano's face drain of all colour. Nano gasped. The letter fluttered to the floor from her trembling hands.

'Nano! What is it?' cried a frightened Ann.

Ann ran forward and threw her arms around her sister, who seemingly had turned to stone. This silence and immobility further alarmed Ann, as it was behaviour so alien to her lively, always animated sister. When there was no response, she disengaged her arms to pick up the letter. Johanna stood transfixed by the bed. Ann, in disbelief, read Uncle Joseph's words:

My dearest nieces,
It is with a heavy heart that I write to inform you that your beloved father, and my dear brother, after a short illness, died at 2 a.m. on the morning of the—

'Oh! Nano! Not Papa! He can't have died!'

Later, the two sisters could not recall the details of that dreadful day. Among the blurred images was that of a black-clad messenger, who had ridden post-haste to their uncle's home with a message from the King, expressing his sorrow at the death of Garrett and his thanks for the years of service he had rendered. The next day the sisters found themselves, together with their aunt and the faithful Johanna, on a boat sailing towards Cork. The influence of their great-uncle Richard had obtained this passage for them. Nano stood on the deck, all thoughts of the pleasures she had once thought she could not live without replaced by a turbulence, like the grey angry waters which hurled themselves hungrily at the boat.

A couple of days later, the four women's eyes searched the wharf, which slowly took shape from the blur of the fog. Yes, there they were – Uncle Joseph, David and Joseph, all dressed in mourning. The ship's bell rang as it approached the wharf. The mooring ropes were unfurled and expertly thrown around the bollards, and the ship came to a gently rocking stop. The women, warmly embraced by the men, smiled wanly. They were led to the waiting coach, which took them to Uncle Joseph's home, where even Nimytwo's eyes were sad.

'My poor dears,' Uncle Joseph sadly murmured. 'After you have all rested I will tell you of our brave Garrett's death.'

The next day, as the mist wound along the river and the channels like gossamer scarfs, the Nagle coach carried Uncle Joseph, Aunt Jane, Nano and Ann to Ballygriffin, where David – now the owner – and their mother Ann awaited their arrival. On their entrance, Nano was roused from her lethargy by the sight of her heartsore mother.

'Poor Mama,' Ann would frequently murmur, during the days which followed.

'Mama, are you sure you want to go to Dublin to live in the house Papa bought?' David asked one morning. 'You know I would love to have you, Nano and Ann stay here,' he continued.

'Thank you, David,' his mother replied, 'but I have made up my mind. I know that one day you will marry that beautiful Mary and bring her here to Ballygriffin, and you will want to raise your family here. Anyway, I think Nano would pine away without her city friends, the balls, and the opera, and darling Ann will go where Nano goes.' She gazed fondly at her eldest son, thinking how proud Garrett would be of him.

In late spring, when the May bush was still in bloom, the Nagle carriage, driven by the now aged Eamon, who refused to relinquish this trip to his son, Connor, his successor, carried Ann and her two daughters to their Dublin home.

'How different it all is from when I left here for school so many years ago,' reflected Nano wistfully. 'I can still feel Papa's warm, firm hand on my elbow.' She sighed and then gazed ahead with determination.

CHAPTER FOUR

Winter soon arrived, and with it came the season of balls. 'Ellen,' called Nano, 'will you find for me that bale of green-patterned silk I brought from Paris? I know I brought quite a few, but I really want the green-patterned one for the dressmaker to make me a gown for next month. I heard that green is all the fashion this year.'

Ellen curtsied as her mother, Molly, had taught her. Molly had married a young man from Killavullen, who worked on the Nagle property. Now that the young Nagle children had grown up, they still lived at Killavullen, in a little cottage Garrett had built for her and her husband. Ellen, their eldest child, was now under the tutorship of Johanna, who was preparing her to become Nano's maid. Ellen went off happily, and searched high and low for the required bale of silk. Disconsolately, she returned with the news that the bale was missing.

Nano frowned thoughtfully. 'Perhaps Miss Ann has seen it,' she concluded. Ann was found sitting in an alcove, quietly reading.

Nano paused. Ann has been looking pale and tired lately, she thought to herself.

To Ann she said, 'Ann, I'm sorry to disturb your reading, but have you seen the green-patterned silk bale I brought from Paris?'

Ann looked up, placed a finger in the page to mark her place, smiled at Nano, and replied, 'Oh, Nano! I really thought you didn't need it, as you have so many gowns. You might not know the Murphys. They live in Saint Michen's parish, and the poor father died with the fever last month, leaving a wife and six little children. They had already lost three children from the fever. They are so poor. I knew you wouldn't like to see them starve, so I asked Mama's maid, Emer, to sell the silk, and we gave the money to the mother for food, clothing and rent. I'm sorry, Nano, but you should have seen the poor little sad, faces break into smiles. You would have been so happy.'

Suddenly, with great clarity, Nano once more saw the tattered shivering group of people at the church door in Paris. She was so transfixed by the stark image that she did not respond for a second or two. Then, realising that Ann was looking at her strangely, she came back to the present and hugged her, saying, 'Ann, you are a darling. I do wish I were thoughtful and brave like you. I didn't realise people were so poor here.'

'I knew you would be happy to save a poor family, even if you didn't know them. I like the golden coloured roll of silk. You would look stunning in that,' Ann suggested.

'You really are wonderful. The golden roll will be perfect.'

For the next few months Nano danced the nights away, and by day could be seen on the arm of the handsome Mr Moylan, the shipping merchant's son, or with the young Mr Bellews, the youngest son of Sir Patrick, or, to the surprise of some, at the opera accompanied by the dashing Joseph Nuttal, grandson of the noted anti-Papist, the Right Honourable Joseph Nuttal, a former Lord Mayor of Dublin. This young man seemed captivated by the witty, light-hearted Miss Nagle. Amidst all this frivolity, Nano would, at inopportune moments, be disturbed by the images of the tear-streaked faces of the Murphy children, or the tattered French crowd. Like a dull, damaged kaleidoscope, the pictures would intrude upon her mind, to be pushed away by the delights of the moment. Then, suddenly, tragedy struck.

'Nano!' Nano was awakened by a white faced Ann. 'Please come! It's Mama!'

Not waiting to see if Nano was following, Ann fled towards her mother's room, where she was met by Johanna, her wise, criss-crossed old face streaming with tears, and an equally distraught Emer. Beside them stood a shocked, bewildered Ellen, twisting and wringing her apron. Nano dashed to the bed, fell on her knees, and took her mother's hand in her own. How cold it was.

'My poor Mama,' whispered Nano.

Some days later she wrote to her French cousins:

Our dear Mama died during the night of 25 January, this year 1748. Ann and I think that she never fully recovered from Papa's death. She seemed to grow frailer each day. I am only just discovering what she did for the poor, not only here, in Dublin, but also in Ballygriffin.

The Dublin Journal, 26 January, paid her a wonderful tribute, describing her as 'a lady of exemplary piety, a faithful wife, a tender affectionate mother, and a most sincere friend.' We know how well this describes her. She not only taught us our faith, but showed us how to live it. She and Papa were so devoted to each other, and Papa relied on her so much while he was away. You know this, because I often heard him speak to you of her, on his frequent visits to France. We knew she had many friends, but we have been consoled by the many who have come to grieve with us.

Your fond cousin,
Nano

On 6 April 1749, when the mourning time had concluded, David's wedding to Mary Harrold took place in the very fashionable Saint Anne's Church in Soho, London, where the

Harrolds had moved from Cork. As he waited for Mary to arrive at the church, David smiled at his beautiful sisters in the front seats. There was Nano, the height of fashion as always, her eyes shining with pleasure; beside her Ann, looking rather fragile, he thought; Mary, dearest Mary, with her husband and their second cousin the widowed Pierce Nagle; then Catherine and 'little' Elizabeth – no longer little of course. Behind them sat his uncles and aunts, including a beaming Uncle Joseph, and a multitude of cousins. Joseph, ramrod straight, impeccably attired, and not a dark curl out of place, stood beside David, a wicked gleam in his dark eyes. What has he been up to now? David wondered anxiously. Thanks be to God Mama never knew that he fought at Fontenoy. David had no more time for reflection. The first chords of one of Johan Helmich Roman's wedding music compositions leapt joyfully through the church, heralding the arrival of his beloved Mary, and on her diminutive, lace-clad figure, his eyes, thoughts and heart turned and remained.

Some months later, Ann was confined to bed, her life slowly ebbing away. On the evening of her death, Nano sat beside the bed, holding her hand, as she had so often done when they were children. Ann stepped quietly and gently into her heavenly home, as quietly and gently as she had stepped through her earthly life. The whole household felt her loss, but none so deeply as Nano. Nano thought often of Ann's devotion to the poor; of her sale of the bale of silk to aid the Murphy family. After Ann's death, Nano returned to Ballygriffin with the hope that her sorrows would be healed. Eventually, Nano decided to respond to the haunting memories by visiting the poorer families around Ballygriffin.

Accompanied by Ellen, she ventured to some of the one-roomed cottages, carrying food and clothing. Everywhere she went, she was appalled by what she saw. Never had she imagined that people could live with so little, and in such conditions. On her return, she would confide to her sister, Catherine, 'The people don't live; they barely survive. I can scarcely look at the children who are mostly skin and bone. And Catherine,' she would continue, 'they are so ignorant. You know poor old Mary Murray died of a fever, and they actually took a corner of the rag they had her wrapped in to bind around the swollen leg of her little grandson. They believed it would cure him! Another thing: her son, Rory, fell over in the mud near her grave, and now sits beside the so-called turf fire, doing nothing, waiting for death, because they believe the fall was a sign he would die before the year's end.'

One day, a frustrated Nano disturbed David while he was looking over the estate finances, which were laid on his desk.

'David,' she complained, 'young Tom refused to take my message to Mallow, because he said it was bad luck. When I asked how on earth that could be, he said that he'd had a crowing rooster at his door, and that meant it was bad luck to travel! Did you ever hear anything like that? When I visit their cottages, which provide basic shelter but no comfort, I see, as I suppose you have, all the lucky charms they hang about – old rusty horseshoes, plants and flowers of this and that. They have very little knowledge of their faith, or of how to pray.'

David nodded sympathetically. 'Their lives are governed by their superstitions. Mary and I are continuing our parents' practice of encouraging the children to go to the hedge school when a master comes, but that is now infrequent, because we are being closely watched. We try to give work to as many of the people as possible, and, as you know, we all help with food and clothing. But I know that is not enough.'

David twirled the quill between his fingers as he gazed sadly at his sister. Poor Nano, he thought. She takes things to heart these days.

Once more, Nano's nights became tormented by disturbing dreams. By day, she felt so helpless. She would love to teach the children, but felt that she did not have the skills. How could she even get the children to come? It was all becoming too much for Nano. How could the people live in such fear and ignorance? It seemed to be always on her mind. One night she awoke suddenly. She had the solution. She would enter a convent to give her life to prayer and penance for the poor people of Ireland. Her cousin, Margaret, who had so often visited them at Ballygriffin, had already entered the Ursulines in France. I'll have to go to the Continent, she thought, because convents are illegal in Ireland. Her mind made up, Nano acted quickly.

The next morning, she began informing her astonished family. David and his wife Mary, who were expecting their first child, looked shocked. 'Are you sure, Nano?' they both asked.

Her three sisters were stunned into silence. Finally, Mary, who had come to visit with her stepson, Patrick, said in an uncertain voice, 'Nano, do you think you should spend more time thinking about this?' Although she tried, she could not imagine Nano in a convent. Joseph roared with laughter, thinking it was one of Nano's jokes.

'Joseph,' Nano chided him, 'I am really serious about this.'

Joseph looked truly contrite as he said, 'My apologies, Nano. Whatever you want to be, you'll be great.' After a pause he added, 'I hope Frances and I can come to visit you once we are married, though.'

Nano gave him a hug, saying, 'Joseph, I will really miss both you and Frances.'

Uncle Joseph gazed at her solemnly with his wise old eyes. 'Nano,' he said, as he took her small hand in his, 'I know you will do what God asks of you.'

Nano's eyes swam with tears. 'Dear Uncle Joseph,' she began, but never finished what she wished to say; her heart was too full of thanks for his love and kindness.

The next few weeks were busy ones for Nano, the whole family and the household, all of whom were involved in Nano's preparation for her departure to the Continent, and her entry into the convent. Her final day in Ireland – perhaps forever, she thought – arrived all too soon. As the ship carried her away from her beloved family, its sails fluttering in the wind, her heart sank. When will I see them again, she wondered. I won't even be there for the birth of David and Mary's child. I won't see Joseph and Frances married. Have I made the right choice?

Putting all these thoughts and questions aside, Nano went below to where Ellen had already prepared her cabin for the voyage. Since both David and Joseph were unable to accompany her, her cousin Pierce, Mary's husband, would be escorting her, and was already settled in the cabin beside her. The time flew too quickly; within a week Nano was a postulant, and Pierce and Ellen had boarded ship for their return to Ireland. Nano tried to fit into the new regime of early rising, the hour's meditation, Mass, sacred reading, lectures, performing one's 'charges' (as the set manual work was called), and learning the monastic rules. It was all in silence, including the meals. Nano was quite overwhelmed, but was determined to devote her life to prayer and penance.

Only a month into this way of life, she was again plagued by dreams. The vision of the Parisian crowd faded, giving way to the children of Cork whose sticklike arms stretched pleadingly out to her. Their parents' hopeless eyes were fixed on her. Usually in her dreams she would flee from them all, but their voices would swell to a chorus chanting 'Nano! Nano! Please!' Eventually, Nano confided her troubles to the Jesuit priest who had been appointed the confessor.

A man of wisdom and patience, he listened intently, then told Nano: 'Sister, God is calling you back to Ireland.'

Nano was reluctant to return. She felt called to do something to help her people, but firmly believed that she could do that best by a life of prayer in the convent.

'Father,' she would answer, 'I know I can't do anything in Ireland to help the people. I'm not a scholar so I couldn't teach. I'm no good at nursing. I don't even like sewing! I just would not know what to do. Sometimes I can't understand the people's speech, and you should see the way some live. It nearly makes me sick.'

Her troubles were compounded further when she heard that the baby so desired by David and Mary had died at birth. Nano struggled to understand why two people who would deeply cherish a baby had been deprived of that gift, while others abandoned or neglected their children or could not care for them. Why, she would ask herself in moments of doubt. At other times she would chide herself with: God knows best. Weeks passed while Nano adamantly refused to consider returning to Ireland, and the desperate calls of the poor haunted her nights.

Eventually the confessor became so concerned that he admonished Nano: 'Sister, you are not happy here. You are not good to yourself or others. You are not being true to, or listening to, God. You must listen to God with the ears of your heart. God is calling you back to Ireland. So, if you want to enter into eternal life with God, to be with your parents and Ann, and if you really desire to help your people, you must leave the convent and return home as soon as you can.'

These words galvanised Nano into action. Some weeks later she was on the ship bound for Cork, where Joseph and Frances were waiting to welcome her into their home in Cove Lane. Nano slipped quietly back into life at Cove Lane. Each morning, accompanied by Ellen, who had resumed her position as Nano's maid, she set out early to Mass at St Finbarr's Church, where she spent some time in prayer. Sometimes during the day, she would accompany Frances on a shopping tour, or in visiting friends or family, particularly David and Mary, who again were expecting a child. On receiving the news that Mary was pregnant, David, who was fearful they would lose this child also, had purchased a town house in Cork, where he bought Mary to be near medical assistance. Often Nano would spend evenings with Frances and Joseph at home, or on their social outings. At other times Nano would make her apologies and be absent from these functions. Both Joseph and Frances would presume that she was at prayer. Nano, however, always accompanied for safety's sake by Ellen, would in reality be walking in the lanes about Cove Lane, or further afield across the river to places such as Philpot's Lane. In dangerous and poverty-stricken areas like Peddler's Alley, Willow Lane, Gould's Lane, Donovan's Lane and Primrose Lane, Nano became a familiar figure. A basket containing food, clothing, bandages, and ointments would always be on her arm. If it was evening, she and Ellen would carry lanterns through the unlit, un-seweraged, rat-infested areas, where cut-throats and villains of all descriptions plied their trades. These outcasts from society, from their hidden, dark shadows, observed with wonder this fearless lady, who went where few dared to go. As the news spread of Miss Nagle's courage, and her dedication to the dispossessed, the shadow people made sure that Nano walked safely through the streets of Cork. A port city of trade and commerce where ships from across the known world berthed, it was notorious for its crime rate – yet Nano walked unharmed by day and by night on her visits to the most needy.

During these walks and her visits to the garrets of the impoverished, she was appalled at the ignorance and poverty, and especially at the plight of the multitude of ragged, unkempt children, many of whom were engaged in petty crime, as were their destitute parents. Here were the people of her nightmares. In certain parts of the city she observed the presence of a number of well-clad children who attended schools.

During one of the social card evenings being held by Joseph and Frances, Nano casually remarked that she had seen children in Peter Street, and wondered who they were and what they did. Joseph replied that they were children who attended a Charity School endowed by a Mrs Sherman.

'Really?' said Nano. 'What do you know about these schools, Joseph?'

Joseph was only too happy to display his knowledge, and began to explain to Nano about the one she saw and the funct-ions of the Charity Schools.

'The one you saw, Nano, clothes and educates ten poor Protestant boys until they are old enough to be apprenticed to a Protestant master. All the Charity Schools will take Catholic children for the sole purpose of educating them to be Protestants. They teach very little except the religion of the Established Church, I am afraid. The better schools do provide some basic instruction in reading, which they do from the Bible, as well as writing and elementary arithmetic.'

Not to be outdone, his friend, John Lawson, introduced the topic of the Charter Schools. An animated discussion took place about the merits and demerits of each system.

'I really think Charter Schools are a greater danger to Catholics,' John said, and went on to explain, 'They specifically state that learning is to be limited to those skills which enable children to perform the most menial tasks, and children are forced to attend daily Divine Service in the church.'

'Is it true that they can forcibly remove Catholic children from their parents to send them away to a Charter School?' Frances queried.

'Unfortunately, yes,' John replied. 'I also know that they have been granted a Royal Charter and are given £1,000 annually by the King, and about £3,000 by Parliament. So there is no lack of finance, and they are obviously well supported by the authorities who govern our land.'

Suddenly Joseph asked curiously, 'Nano, how did you come to be in an area where these schools are?'

Before Nano could answer, Frances interjected, 'Don't you think, Joseph that we should finish our game, as it is getting late, and our guests will wish to go home soon?' Much to Nano's relief, all agreed enthusiastically.

The next day, however, when Joseph had gone to Dublin on business, Frances questioned Nano on where she was and what she did on her long absences from the house. When Nano disclosed what she had been doing, Frances exclaimed in horror, 'Oh! Nano! Do be careful! Even having Ellen with you is no protection. I read every day in the paper, and I'm sure you do too, of the thieves and murderers who frequent the streets. Some citizens disappear and are never seen again. There are always warnings about being in the streets at night because there is no lighting, as you well know, and people continue to fall into the river and channels where they drown, or are swept out to sea, their bodies never being recovered. I don't know what Joseph would say if he knew what you are doing.'

'Frances, I'm so pleased I can share this with you,' replied Nano, 'I really can't explain to you under what terrible conditions the people live. It's so difficult for me not to hold a handkerchief over my nose when I go into their attics, or for that matter when I walk down the lanes, where everything is thrown. The poor people can never have a wash because there is no water, and whole families live in one room. Most of them are almost starving and are clothed in rags. Sometimes members of the family are ill with fevers. Oh! Dear Frances, it would tear your heart to see them. None of them have ever been to school. Often I can't understand their speech, although sometimes Ellen can, but they understand that I care for them and have come to help. We take food, and Ellen takes some of my unused clothes to a dressmaker to be remade for them. I wish I could do more. Can you think of anything, Frances?'

Frances was silent. At first she had been disbelieving, then shocked, and now she was filled with admiration as she looked at her sister-in-law.

'Nano, I don't think we should tell Joseph just yet. I will find a way to tell him when I think he is ready to hear about your work. We both know how generous he and David are. Thank you for confiding in me, but please be careful, and tell me when you are going out. You must take whatever food you need from the kitchens. I will tell Kate, the cook, to set food aside for you to take, and I will see what we can do about clothing. I really don't know what else we can do.'

Early in the month of July, the door of the house swung open as Joseph strode through, calling out 'Good news! Good news! Frances! Nano! Where are you?' Both women hurried towards the entrance where a jubilant Joseph greeted them with 'It's a boy! David and Mary have a fine boy. Frances, tell the butler to bring some whiskey for me, as well as whatever you and Nano would like. We must have a toast.' It was an evening of celebrations for the long-awaited heir.

A couple of days later, on 14 July 1752, the family attended Saint Finbarr's Church for the baptism of Garrett Joseph Nagle, who opened his eyes in astonishment as the waters of baptism splashed on his head. Little Garrett slept through the festivities which followed. Doting parents, uncles and aunts hovered around his cradle, as though expecting him to disappear at any moment.

Mary, still tired from the birth, smilingly said, 'David, I think he will have hair like your father's, Nano's and Joseph's, but I'm sure his eyes are like yours, and I pray he will be as wonderfully kind as you.'

David's eyes spoke many things which only Mary could understand. Joseph proudly preened himself and Nano's eyes sparkled in appreciation.

Nano continued her daily walks to the attics and hovels of the poor. Each day she passed the Blue Coat Charity School, or the Green Coat School for boys in the Shandon Parish. These schools were part of the Charity School movement. Nano now knew that each school with its distinctive uniform was set up by philanthropic individuals to teach children reading, writing and the principals of the Established Church of Ireland. Their whole purpose was to make the whole nation Protestant and English.

A few weeks after little Garrett's baptism, the Nagle house in Cove Lane was awakened by the terrible news that the baby had died unexpectedly during the night. Joseph, Frances, Nano and Catherine hastened to David's house in the South Mall to console the devastated parents. They were soon joined by Uncle Joseph, then Elizabeth, and finally Mary and Pierce. It was a day that would remain ever etched in their memories, particularly as David and Mary were to have no more children. Only their deep faith in the constant love of God was to sustain them.

Life, as it always does, continued for the Nagle family. Nano's first personal experience of the Charter Schools occurred on a visit to a particularly destitute hovel. That evening she described the harrowing scene to Frances and to her sister Catherine, who had come to live in Georges Quay, and was now familiar with Nano's work with the poor. While they were at supper and the servants had retired, Frances, who had been covertly observing Nano remarked, 'Nano, you do seem quiet tonight. Are you tired?'

Nano looked up, a smile transforming her face. 'Frances, you notice everything.'

She glanced at both women before making up her mind to share with them the happenings of the day.

'Well, truth be told I did have a harrowing day,' she began. 'It was so dreadfully sad, I don't know where to begin. I think I have mentioned before that I visit a poor little Walsh family who live in Primrose Lane. You remember, the father died last year leaving a mother and five small children, including a baby of about twelve months – although it looks about six months it is so malnourished. The two eldest, eight-year-old Rory together with little seven-year-old Danny, scavenge for food for them all. This morning when Ellen and I went up the rickety steps to where they live, poor Mrs Walsh and the little girls were all rocking back and forth and weeping with grief. We finally discovered that the problem was that the two boys, together with some other boys and girls from the nearby lanes, had been snatched by the agents of the Charter Schools. They had been taken away to the country to be educated as Protestants, and apprenticed to Protestant masters. I remember Joseph's friend, Mr Lawson, said there are three or four such schools in County Cork. I really could not console the family. It was heart-rending. All I could do was leave them food and clothing and promise to come again. There must be some way we can halt these terrible happenings.'

Her two listeners were visibly troubled. Catherine sighed, and eventually said, 'Nano, if I can do anything at all to help, please let me know. I really can't think of anything at the moment, but Mama always said our first step is to pray and then perhaps we will find an answer.'

'Yes,' added Frances, 'we will certainly do that. I wish I could find an appropriate time to talk to Joseph, but at the moment he is so busy with property issues and is home so late that I have been unable to talk to him about your work, Nano.'

'Thank you both so much for your support. It is such a relief to be able to share with you,' Nano replied.

Concerned about Nano's health, Frances and Catherine decided that a few days in Dublin would benefit them all. It did not take long to convince Nano that such a visit would be most enjoyable, especially when Catherine told Nano of a wonderful young dressmaker who was interested in improving the situation of poor children near where she lived in Dublin.

'I think you will like her, Nano,' Catherine said, 'and you must admit you do need some new clothes.'

Joseph Nagle's coach soon had them in Dublin where the women lost no time in visiting the long list of family friends. There followed walks in Phoenix Park where they met other wealthy Irish, and another day they were driven past Jonathan Swift's newly built Saint Patrick's Church. The evening before they left, they attended the Great Music Hall in Fishamble Street, where Handel's *Messiah*, which was again being played, having been first performed in Lent 1742. The three women enjoyed every minute of the visit, but for Nano perhaps the most memorable part was their visit to the young dressmaker, Teresa Mulally. Although Nano was ten years older than Teresa, the two women immediately felt a rapport. Teresa, an only child, lived with her parents and ran a thriving business, established with the money she had inherited from an aunt with whom she had lived for two years in Chester. A talented businesswoman, Teresa was able to support her elderly parents and contribute to the alleviation of the poverty of those who lived in the vicinity. When the three women left the Mulally household, Nano and

Teresa promised to stay in touch. Thus began a lifelong friendship, maintained mainly through correspondence and a common purpose of serving the underprivileged.

CHAPTER FIVE

As the sight of Charity School children filing into their schools or churches became familiar to Nano, gradually an idea began to germinate in her mind. Each morning when she knelt at prayer in Saint Finbarr's, she talked to her beloved God about her problem, and her emerging plan.

'You know I didn't want to come back to Cork, and I am only here because it is what you wanted of me. I have been dreaming your dream of a different world for the people. I think the only way to improve the people's lives is to give them an education. I know what it has done for us and I saw what the Little Schools did in France. If I can give the people knowledge and skills they will be able to obtain work and can improve their lives. If I can teach them their faith they will be free from the superstitions which entangle their lives in fear and dread. Everyday I see the Charity and Charter Schools for the Protestant children, or those they wish to make Protestant, so why can't I have a school for Catholic children? I know I have never been a scholar, but I know about our faith, so perhaps I can employ some women to teach while I can tell children about our faith. I know, too, that the law forbids schools for or by Catholics, which is totally unjust. I absolutely abhor injustices. They really infuriate me. I've thought of a way I could escape detection, but how can I get the children to attend? I wonder if that is what you want of me? If I try and it succeeds, I will know that is your will – so I'm going to try. I'll leave the rest in your hands, dear God.'

Nano continued to pray and to think through her plans. Having made a decision, she spoke to her confessor, who was known for his selfless dedication to the poor. He gave her his support, but warned her of the possible consequences of taking such a dangerous action. Undeterred, Nano's first step was to purchase a small cottage in Cove Lane at a place where children naturally gathered, and near to the Blue Coat Charity School. She would disguise the cottage to look like a baker's shop, and would make sure that there would always be a spotter to warn of trouble. Choosing teachers was far more challenging. While the carpenters, plasterers and thatchers were renovating the cottage, Nano carefully selected a young woman to help her in the instruction of the girls she would take into her school. Any teacher she chose would need to be well educated, compassionate, committed to the Catholic faith and to teaching. I don't agree with the belief that teachers of the poor need only a basic education, she thought. I'll make sure my teachers have a very good education. In the mornings she would impart knowledge of their faith and its practices to the children, and in the afternoons the teacher would instruct them in writing, reading, arithmetic and sewing. Nano had a well-planned curriculum. Drawing on her own experiences in the hedge school and in France, together with what she had heard about the French Little Schools and the lively conversations in which she had taken part in the French salons, Nano devised her school curriculum, which was to differ markedly from those of other schools of that era. When all was ready, Nano sent Ellen and Josephine, a teacher she had employed, into the laneways to offer the opportunity of schooling to thirty poor ragged girls.

Nano's school was an immediate success. Her compassion and enthusiasm drew the children like a magnet, although she would never forget her first encounter with them.

'I was absolutely terrified,' she was to say later. 'They were like little gnome monstrosities, their filthy clothes in tatters, and their language indescribable.'

At the end of the first week Nano said to her young teacher, 'Josephine, we cannot expect the children to learn while they are scratching with vermin and are starving. Tomorrow we will bring food and clothing to give them before we start classes. Whatever you buy I will see that you receive reimbursement. I wonder what we can do to help them become cleaner?'

Josephine pondered the question for some seconds before replying, 'You know my brother Kevin? I hope you don't mind but I've shared with him what we do, as I know he is so discreet, and he really supports all our efforts. He also loves adventure, so would you agree that I ask him to purchase some buckets from the merchant on the corner and to fill them with clean water? Unlike these poor people, we have access to clean water; their only option is getting water from the river, which is so filthy. He would love to bring the buckets around, and no one will ask a young man why he is carrying water. He could wear his worst clothes to allay any suspicions. People will probably think he is a servant getting water for his master.'

'It seems a solution to our problem, Josephine, but I don't want to endanger your brother's life. It would be terrible if he were caught supporting a Catholic school. I could never forgive myself if he were found out and hanged, or imprisoned and sent to the American colonies as a slave.'

Josephine chuckled. 'Miss Nagle, you don't know our Kevin. My mother is always worried he will be caught for some of his activities, but our father says he is too smart for that. He is a great actor and mimic. He has already managed to help some priests who would not take the Oath of Abjuration to escape. You will meet him tomorrow if you agree.'

Nano spent a sleepless night imagining the hapless Kevin carted away in chains, while his mother wept inconsolably. The next morning, however, she was met at the door of her school by a very disreputable-looking young man, carrying two buckets of water, who spoke to her in a broad dialect. It was only when she looked into his roguish brown eyes that she realised this was Kevin in his disguise. Kevin deposited the buckets inside the doorway, and after a quick scan of the street greeted Nano in a cultured voice. He promised to return at the end of the day to collect and refill the buckets for the following morning. Kevin was one of the many who were to assist Nano in her work over the years.

That morning when the girls arrived there were screams of fright and panic as Nano and Josephine began to wash their faces and hands. The children were terrified that their skin would fall off, or that perhaps they would drown; after all, they had heard of people drowning in the waters of the river. Soon their fears were allayed, and they laughed with glee and amazement as they gazed at each other's faces devoid of grime and dirt. The next morning they were competing to see who was the prettiest. Clad in their clean pinafores, and at least clean in spots, and fortified with the bread and soup with which they were fed at school, most of the children began to learn quickly.

Each day, Nano arrived with pictures and symbols of Catholic faith, wrapped in little parcels like food and placed in her basket. Josephine did likewise with her slates and slate pencils, or at other times with Bibles, reading matter or sewing materials. Each day more little girls arrived, each cleaner than the first group. Soon the room was almost overflowing with the girls, posing another problem for Nano. What could she do about this? Surely it would be too risky to begin another school, and if she did how could she finance it? Could she ask another teacher to risk so much and to join her in this dangerous work? While she was pondering these questions, she was also thinking over the way in which the children were learning.

One afternoon when the children had gone home, Nano discussed the latter issue with Josephine. 'I have observed, as you no doubt have, Josephine, that each child learns differently and at a different pace. Some grasp the facts and learn the skills very quickly, while others take much longer. I have been wondering about this. I know it is the general practice that all the children repeat and repeat until everyone knows what is being taught, or else the majority know and move on, and the others never learn and are left far behind. I think we could try adapting our teaching to the way the different children learn. We could let the quick learners move on, but be very patient with those who are slower, and revise with them and give them time until they are ready to move. Do you think we could try that?'

Her young teacher nodded enthusiastically. She would try anything to please her wonderful Miss Nagle.

'Miss Nagle, it is difficult for us too, to see children losing confidence by being left behind. I also find it very boring to teach reading only from the Bible as the other schools do. It's really cruel to expect little Fidelma to learn as quickly as Maeve, who seems very bright. Yesterday I saw poor little Fidelma, her tongue out, her forehead furrowed with worry as she tried to stitch straight for so long, while Maeve's was perfect in very little time. I'm sure she will be able to make a petticoat for herself soon. Like you, Miss Nagle, I can't wait until the time our children are skilled and confident enough to get work.'

Nano continued to spend her mornings at her school, and her afternoons and many of her evenings visiting the lanes and attics where she attended to the sick, provided food for the abandoned and gave hope and comfort to the depressed. This busy life continued for her until one evening when she, Frances and Joseph were gathered for their evening meal, and a loud persistent knocking was heard at the door. The servant who answered came in and said to Joseph, 'There's a poor man at the door who insists on seeing you, sir.'

With an apology to the women, Joseph followed the servant to the door, where there stood a shabbily but cleanly dressed man, cap in hand.

'Now, my man, what do you want at this hour of the night?' Joseph asked kindly.

'Mr Nagle, sir,' the man spoke softly, nervously twisting the cap in his hand. 'Sir, I've come to ask if you would take my little girl into the school your sister, Miss Nagle, runs in Cove Lane?'

Joseph opened his mouth, then quickly closed it. He felt like laughing, but the poor man looked at him so pleadingly, he searched for a compassionate way to dismiss him.

Mistaking Joseph's silence for indecision, the man said again, 'She's only a wee girl, but good, sir, and we'll make sure that she learns her lessons.'

By this stage Joseph had collected his thoughts and kindly dismissed the man, assuring him that he was mistaken because no such school was run by Miss Nagle, but he commended him for his interest in his children's education.

When Joseph returned to the dining room he could no longer contain his mirth, as he recounted the conversation to Frances and Nano. There was silence. Frances looked inquiringly at Nano. Surely even Nano would not dare, she thought. Nano broke the silence in a soft but firm voice.

'Joseph, what you heard is true.' As she saw Joseph's face redden and felt his anger rising, she hastily described to him her purchase of the cottage, the establishment of her school and its success. She also told him of her visits to the lost in the lanes and alleyways.

Joseph's mounting anger burst forth.

'Nano!' he roared. 'What have you done? How can you be so foolish! And thoughtless! Didn't you think about what could happen to Frances and me, if we were investigated? You know the law about anyone who fought for the French and returned to Ireland. You know very well men who served with the Irish Brigade have been executed. Only last week I spoke about Denis Dunne's execution. Would you like to see me killed? All our family could lose our lands, our goods, even our lives. You might not care about yourself, but I care about us all. What about Uncle Joseph? He has had enough investigations without this. What do you think he's going to say when he hears about this latest escapade of yours!'

In the brief pause which followed this outburst, Frances said gently, 'Now Joseph, please don't be so angry. I'm sure Nano hasn't been reckless.'

Joseph ignored this comment. 'Nano,' he shouted not quite so loudly, 'tomorrow you and I are going to Uncle Joseph about this foolishness of yours. Be ready by eleven o'clock,' he ordered.

'Yes, Joseph,' Nano quietly acquiesced. As her eyes were cast down, neither of her listeners could observe the determined glint they bore.

A very subdued meal followed, with Nano and Frances conversing quietly at intervals, while Joseph continued to glower at Nano.

The next day Joseph, Nano and Frances were welcomed by Uncle Joseph with his usual affectionate smile – but on seeing Joseph's scowling face he raised an inquisitive eyebrow at Nano. He didn't have to wait long before Joseph angrily described what he thought was Nano's latest ill-conceived escapade.

Uncle Joseph sat and listened attentively without interrupting his nephew. He then turned to Nano.

'Would you like to say anything, Nano?' He asked gently.

'Yes, I would,' replied Nano just as gently. She recounted how, because she feared for them all, she had set about her work quietly, methodically and in secret. She had taken all the precautions she could think of. Her little school, she said, was sought after by so many that it was no longer sufficient. It was so transformative that she would like to open more schools for girls, but in such disreputable and poor areas that the authorities would never dream a school could exist.

'Dear Uncle Joseph,' she concluded, 'I know it is dangerous work, but I believe it is what God wants, and I place all my trust in him to keep us all safe, particularly if I do my part. I pray, Uncle Joseph, that you will give me your blessing.'

'Nano,' Uncle Joseph paused, then continued, 'Nano, never let it be said that a Nagle was too afraid to do what he or she believed was right. You believe that this is God's work, so you must continue. If ever you need anything you must let us know.'

Before Nano could reply he turned to Joseph. 'My boy, you have never been afraid to fight for what you believed in, and now Nano is doing the same. Thank you, my boy, for bringing Nano today.'

A now pacified and relieved Joseph smiled his thanks, while Nano, grateful for her uncle's support, went to him and hugged him.

Later that afternoon after a happy Joseph had returned to work, Frances said to Nano, 'It is very dangerous work you are doing, but of course we will all support you. Please consider taking little boys into your school. I keep thinking of David's little sons, and of the sons Joseph and I have never had and perhaps never will. It makes me so sad. If you take little boys it will alleviate my sorrows somewhat and I will certainly give all I can to help.'

'Yes, I know it is dangerous,' Nano confessed, and for a moment looked truly fearful. 'I have to do it, Frances,' she continued, 'I am sure that is what God wants of me. I have prayed and prayed, and thought and thought, and now I must continue to act.' She smiled teasingly at Frances as she went on. 'It is a relief to have the family support and because I can see you are about to withdraw yours if I don't take boys, I'll have a school for them, too.'

Although Nano was busy working with the destitute and always dreaming of new ways to help them, she was never too preoccupied to be involved in family life. She had watched Catherine's deteriorating health with concern, and spent as much time as she could with her. When she had first become aware that Catherine was ill she had discussed the problem with Joseph and Mary, both of whom shared her apprehensions about Catherine's health, and tried to ease Catherine's discomfort. As their efforts proved futile, Nano and Frances travelled in Joseph's coach across to Ballygriffin where they consulted with David about the best course of action to be taken.

'Perhaps, David,' Nano suggested 'We could take Catherine to France to our cousins for a holiday. I'm sure all of our relatives in France would be overjoyed to see us, and it would be warmer and dryer in France.'

David, always quiet and undemonstrative, looked with sympathy at Nano and Frances.

'You remember when Mary and I were in Cork at our town house a few weeks back, I spoke to Catherine about her health. Mary accompanied her to the best physician in Cork, who said there was little we could do beyond what we were doing to ease her life. We left it to Catherine to tell you both, and Joseph, when she was ready to do so. She has hesitated to do so when you have so many other problems, Nano, and if she told you, Frances, Nano can read your face so well, she would become more concerned than ever. I'm really sorry, especially for you, Nano. It is so difficult to see a younger sibling suffer and die. You have already keenly felt the death of Ann, and now face another death. We are fortunate in that we have a supportive and faith-filled family.'

The next day Catherine told the family in Cove Lane the doctor's diagnosis, saying she was not afraid to die, but hoped she would not become a burden to them. Frances wept silently and Nano thought sadly of the little golden-haired baby with the beautiful smile. She still has her golden hair, she mused, her heart desolate, and how I will miss her beautiful smile. Joseph blinked away his tears, gave Catherine a hug and marched into his study, closing the door quietly behind him.

It was on a cold, crisp morning in 1754 when the breath of the gentle breeze stirred the grasses and the dew hung like pearl teardrops from the trees that the family gathered to bury Catherine beside her parents, her sister Ann and nephew Garrett Joseph. Nano felt an overwhelming sadness as the coffin disappeared from sight. Once more the grieving family gathered at Ballygriffin to support each other, and to reminisce on the happy family days they had experienced.

The following day, David and Mary sadly watched the carriages take the family members down the driveway, through the iron gates and back to their homes. As they turned to go inside David expressed his worries to Mary about Uncle Joseph. Mary, putting her arm through David's replied, 'David, he is a very old man, and we have lost so many family members whom he has loved deeply. Also none of us know of the many cases of injustices that he is trying to right, and of course he is always in danger of facing investigations into his work for Catholics, and indeed into Nagle properties and their use. I am afraid all we can do is to care and pray for him, and to try not to become embroiled in any lawsuits ourselves. Since our parents managed to do that so well, so we can too. Although Nano's work is dangerous she is very astute, so I don't think Uncle Joseph will be worried about her, and he does support her in everything.'

CHAPTER SIX

Within nine months of opening her first school, the number of children Nano was educating had risen to two hundred. For Nano, there was only one option: she would need to open more schools that would operate under her system of education. First she opened a school for boys, as requested by Frances. She did this near her girls' school and the Blue Coat Charity School for boys, and employed a master to teach them. As with her female teachers, she made certain that he was well educated and had a love of and commitment to his students. Although there were a number of small schools, hidden like Nano's, which educated Catholic boys in preparation for seminaries on the Continent (and which one had to be rich enough to afford fees to attend), no one before had ever dared dream of establishing a system of education for the urban poor – or for anyone else for that matter. No one before had ever dreamed of a system educating the poor for the whole of life, for being able to better their situation and improve their lives, free from superstition and fear, where they would form a relationship with a caring creator. No one had ever dreamed of establishing a system educating and empowering girls so that they could provide for themselves and live independent lives.

At a dinner party held one evening at David and Mary's town house and from which Uncle Joseph was absent because of illness, the conversation turned to Nano's schools.

'So, I've heard that you have opened a school. Do tell us about what you do,' Mrs Gould asked.

Nano hesitated before replying carefully. 'I have gone about it all very quietly. I started with a girls' school because I saw how vulnerable poor girls are, particularly orphan girls and the children of prostitutes. Now, because Frances suggested it, I have established a school for poor boys. Both schools are in Cove Lane, and both are overflowing.'

'It's wonderful when one thinks of the struggle other schools for the poor have to retain students. Most of them never reach forty students, and they usually close in a short time,' Joseph boasted proudly.

'Did I hear that the people around The Shambles on the north side of the river are also asking for schools?' queried Mr Gould.

'Oh! You surely wouldn't go there!' interjected Mrs Gould.

'No, of course she wouldn't,' Mr Gould answered decisively.

He turned to David, 'David, you must have heard of the crime rate in the alleys off Fair Lane and Mallow Lane. You know Mallow Lane is infamous as the city's nursery of villainy. You know that the people there who work in the slaughter yards have as little regard for human life as for the beasts they slaughter.'

'True,' answered David.

'Talking of slaughter yards,' said Joseph, aware of Nano's plans and eager to change the subject, 'how is the shipping trade for you these days, Mr Gould?'

To the relief of the family, the ploy worked. The men launched into a discussion on the dangers and profits of trade, with an occasional added comment from the women on the importation of silks and lace from France.

'We know it is illegal,' said Frances, 'but as we don't make them here in Ireland, what are we to do?'

The other women nodded in agreement.

'We can't complain about your silks and lace, because we enjoy the brandy, and of course the claret,' laughed Joseph.

When the last of the guests had gone, David turned to Mary, saying, 'Thank God for Joseph. I was wondering for how long we could avoid telling our guests about Nano's plans.'

'Yes,' Mary replied. 'I was afraid someone would start talking about North Gate Prison and its inhabitants. It's such a terrible place. I sometimes think the jailers are worse than those who are jailed. Fortunately we know she won't get involved in trying to help them. Remember how afraid she was of the children when she began her first school? And these people are far, far worse.'

'Who knows what Nano will dare,' David replied thoughtfully, before continuing, 'We must visit Uncle Joseph tomorrow. I am fearful of his failing health, Mary.'

Nano gradually bought cottages on each side of the river to accommodate the number of children coming to her schools. As had become her practice, she supervised their restoration. When the weather was wet and cold she cautioned the workmen. 'Yes, I know that I asked you to finish the work quickly, but you must let the plaster dry before you take the next step. It's more important to have the building well constructed than to be finished on time.'

On arriving home, Joseph, who had been visiting the building near Philpot Lane, laughingly said to Frances, 'If only Mama could see Nano now. She used to be so cross when, instead of going to lessons, Nano would stay watching the workmen building a barn. Now, because she did, she knows what the men should be doing with the restoration of the cottages.'

Nano's interest in builders extended beyond the quality of their work to their working conditions. Before beginning her building programme, she had inquired about wages and working hours by asking Joseph what happened on other buildings. She was aghast at what they discovered.

'Do you mean, Joseph, that the men can be required to work as long as the owner wants and he can pay them what he thinks they deserve?'

'Sadly that seems so,' replied Joseph. 'Moreover, if the money runs out they might be paid nothing at all.'

'That is outrageous!' exclaimed Nano. 'I'll go to see Uncle Joseph and we'll work out a fair deal for my workers.'

A week later Nano met with her workers to inform them of the new arrangements: a just wage for honest workers, and hours which allowed time for families to be together. The results were astounding. The workers had the buildings finished on time and to Nano's satisfaction. Now aware of their rights, many of the workmen were empowered to seek better conditions for themselves.

In early 1757 after one of Nano's visits to Uncle Joseph, the family was summoned to Blackrock where Uncle Joseph lay dying. Nano, her eyes burning with unshed tears, sat holding his hand as this great man said farewell to his family. On that bleak day in 1757 as the black-plumed horses drew the hearse carrying Uncle Joseph's body to its resting place, crowds lined the streets with their heads bowed. The one who suffered his loss most was Nano, acknowledged by all to be his favourite. I will never hear his voice again, she whispered to herself. I will never again see his kind, twinkling eyes. I will never be able to seek his advice. There would forever be that little ache in her heart for her parents, darling Ann, golden-haired Catherine and her dearest Uncle Joseph. In time she would be able to thank God for the gifts of their lives, for the gifts they shared – but not yet.

The following year, on 7 February 1758, the family gathered in The Bishops Chapel, Cork, for a celebratory event: Elizabeth's marriage to Robert French. A day of rejoicing followed the marriage of the youngest member of the Nagle family. It was a fashionable affair which was reported in the *Cork Evening Post* of 9 February 1758. Elizabeth was described as 'an agreeable lady with a fortune of £12,000'. The groom came from a wealthy Catholic landowning family from near Craughwell, County Galway. The Nagle brothers and Nano were pleased and relieved that their 'little' Elizabeth's future seemed assured.

After Elizabeth and Robert departed for their home in Galway, Joseph and Frances broke the news to Nano that they were preparing to move to Hollyhill, north of Dublin. At the news Nano felt doubly bereft. She did not reveal her true feelings to them both, as she recognised Joseph's need for the move.

'I will miss you both terribly,' she said. 'You have always been there for me and have shared my joys and sorrows. I'll really miss our talks and discussions, and the advice you so often gave me. I'll especially miss our evenings together. It will be lonely coming home to a house without you.'

Joseph's eyes were unusually serious as he said, 'Nano, I do wish you would come with us; there'll be a hole in our lives without you. But, I know you won't leave your work here.'

'What will I do without you, Nano! You will never know how much I have appreciated your presence. Please do come to visit us as often as you can,' Frances pleaded.

The solemn atmosphere of the house was broken the next day, when, on Nano's return from her hour's prayer in Saint Finbarr's and her school rounds, Frances told her there was a letter for her from Dublin. Nano's tired face brightened as she saw the writing. Hastily she broke open the seal. It was so long since she had heard from her friend, Teresa Mulally.

Dear Miss Nagle,

I have read in the papers the news of your Uncle Joseph's death, and as you always spoke so lovingly of him and felt a special bond with him, I am expressing my sorrow at your deep loss.

Then I was happy to read of your sister Elizabeth's marriage to that fine young man Mr French, of whom you spoke with affection. I pray that they have a life of happiness together.

My parents' health is not as good as I would wish. Although at the present my business is doing well, I was facing a struggle to assist them financially for many years. Now I am happy to share the news with you that I have recently won a state lottery of a few hundred pounds. God is so good. I can now expand my business, as well as provide comfort for my parents.

I am sorry to say that the poverty around these areas never lessens, and the poor children – ragged, starving and uneducated – are doomed to a life of criminality and early death. As my mother has done before me, I do try to help with food and clothing when I can.

I am hoping I hear from you soon about your family and your work.

Your affectionate friend,
Teresa Mulally

Nano passed the letter to Frances, who exclaimed with pleasure over Teresa's good fortune.

'Before we move, Nano, why don't you invite Teresa to spend a few days with us?'

'Thank you, Frances, it would be a joy to have her visit. Although she is rather quiet, she is such a cheerful and bright person, it would perhaps be good for us all,' Nano replied.

To their delight, it wasn't long before Teresa arrived. Frances and Nano showed her the better parts of Cork, and visited David and Mary who, having leased Ballygriffin, were in town; however, they avoided showing her the fetid lanes, especially those on the north side of the Lee. Some days after her arrival, Teresa asked Nano if she could visit one of her schools. Nano, recognising Teresa's sincerity, decided to take her to her boys' schools in Cove Lane and to a girls' on the north side of the river.

As the women left the house and walked through the streets, Nano advised Teresa to lift her skirts and watch carefully where she walked. 'Be aware that there might be slops thrown from above – or worse,' Nano warned.

Teresa did as Nano suggested, saying as she did so, 'Unfortunately, it isn't much better in parts of Dublin. The population there is increasing as the impoverished and landless drag themselves across the country looking for work, of which there is very little for those without skills. I suppose it is the same here,' Teresa commented.

'Indeed it is,' Nano sighed. Before she could elaborate they reached the door of her school, where a 'lookout' child ushered them into the house. Teresa gasped in surprise. Before her were many little boys, neatly dressed, fairly clean and all happily engaged in learning. Some had catechisms in their hands, others slates on which they wrote, albeit some laboriously, with their slate pencils.

'What are those older boys doing?' asked Teresa when they moved into another room.

Nano smiled proudly. 'Why don't you ask Connor?' she replied.

Connor looked up shyly from a piece of cloth he was stitching and said something so softly that, although Teresa strained to hear, the words were a jumble.

'Now, Connor,' said Nano, 'I know you can speak beautifully. Don't be afraid to tell Miss Mulally what you are doing.'

Reassured, Connor explained, 'We are learning sailmaking, miss. I'm going to get a job on the ships so I can help my mam and my brothers and sisters.'

Teresa was so enthralled by what was happening that they spent several hours there, meaning it was too late to visit a girls' school that day. At home that evening Nano explained how the boys learnt their prayers, reading, writing and arithmetic, as well as skills like basic navigation and sailmaking.

'This is such a busy port for trade that I thought if the boys learnt skills based around ships and shipbuilding, they would be able to obtain work. Better still, if they are good enough, they will be able to set up their own businesses and raise themselves out of the ranks of the powerless,' Nano explained to Teresa.

'Some people would be threatened by that idea,' Teresa remarked. 'Most believe when you are born into a place in society that's where you stay.'

'Well, I certainly don't believe that,' Nano remarked shortly. 'I also believe it is unjust not to assist people when one can.'

'Nano, you could land yourself in terrible trouble by educating all those little Catholic boys and girls. I suppose you have heard that many times. How do you avoid being caught at your work?'

'I have been very careful where I have my schools, and have gone about it all slowly. Plus, you saw how Connor was reluctant to speak about what was happening? Everyone involved has learnt to be careful.' After a pause, she smiled mischievously and said, 'I know this sounds cynical, but I suspect that the authorities and those with power and money are so happy to have their property safer, with so many little thieves, pickpockets and arsonists off the streets, that they ignore what I am doing.'

The next day the women made a visit to a girls' school which was equally well hidden. Here Teresa saw girls of all ages, like the boys, learning prayers, reading, writing and basic arithmetic. Instead of sailmaking the girls were learning various sewing stitches through making garments, not samplers, as Nano believed they could learn better in this more practical way.

'I educate all my teachers to be good teachers, and expect them to be devoted to their faith, their work and their students. I also reserve the teaching of religion to myself and I spend time in each of the schools every day.'

Teresa returned thoughtfully to Dublin. She was to reflect on the experience as she watched the ragged, and what some people labelled 'wicked', children who inhabited the lanes around Mary Street in Dublin.

It seemed to Nano no time at all until she said goodbye to Joseph and Frances and moved into a little cottage not far from her school. There was now a greater worry weighing on her shoulders. The money from her great fortune was not easily accessible. Uncle Joseph was no longer there to help her, and there were no family members in Cork with whom she could discuss her financial problems. For some days it was a burden which she carried as she struggled to meet all her commitments. What am I thinking, she said to herself one morning. How could I be so foolish! When has God ever abandoned me? Never! Later that morning as she knelt in St Finbarr's Church, Nano poured out her worries to God. 'It's your work,' she said. 'You love all these children, so I am depending totally on you to provide. You always have and I know you always will.' When Nano left the church after her conversation with God, her heart felt at peace. It came as no surprise to her to hear soon after that her brothers, Elizabeth and she had each received the sum of £1,433 eleven shillings and five pence from a settlement of some of Uncle Joseph's affairs. Unfortunately, on account of the Penal

Laws, Catholics were forbidden to make wills, so Uncle Joseph's total legacy was unavailable until long after Nano's death.

CHAPTER SEVEN

With each day Nano became more aware of the plight of impoverished women. They seemed to be everywhere, begging on the street, prostituting day and night. Why were there so many, she at first wondered. Contact with the children in her schools and with the women themselves soon gave her the answer. Work accidents in the slaughter yards, death from the frequent street brawls, raids by press gangs forcing men into army or naval service, disease, famine and drunkenness all added to the early death of many men. Uneducated and unable to find work, many women were forced into soliciting in order to survive, or to provide for their children. Nano pondered the question of what to do about these women whose lives of degradation were derided and despised, and usually cut short through disease. It pained her to read the newspapers describing them as 'certain shocking objects infesting the city'. People were warned to avoid them in places such as Pikes Lane, Wisdom's Lane and in the network of alleys around Hammonds Marsh.

Her education of girls would help, Nano reflected, but she desired to do more. Each time she read of these women, or met them in the streets or ministered to their ills and sores in the hovels, she was confronted by the question of what to do for them. The prevalence of violence against women, especially the poor and unprotected, alarmed and saddened her. The reports of rapes, strangling, stabbings and other forms of murder of women were common.

One dark, stormy evening as she walked home, clutching her cloak in one hand and her lantern in the other, in the lantern beams she caught sight of a poor prostitute woman soliciting two drunken sailors. Unable to do anything but say a silent prayer for her, she struggled against the wind to the safety of her own home. It was only when she reached the door and opened it that an inspiration came to her. Suddenly, there flashed through her memory the image of so many home-comings when she was young. She felt the warmth, saw the well-clad family with their lace collars and cuffs, and even sometimes the women in their lace shawls. Lace. That was the answer. Why hadn't she thought of lace before? In churches it was on the altar and on some priests' vestments. In Paris it was so fashionable, but in Ireland it had to be imported, or often smuggled in. Lacemaking – I will add it to the curriculum, Nano thought. Moreover, I will offer classes for girls and young women after school, and in that way they will develop a skill which can be used all their lives. The more she thought about it, the more advantages she saw. After classes they will be going home in groups and in that way will be more protected from street gangs. In time, they may earn enough money to set up their own businesses from their homes.

A few days later when David and Mary came to town, Nano shared with them her ideas.

'Nano, I think it is an absolutely wonderful idea, but it will take a lot of money, won't it?' Mary asked anxiously.

David smilingly observed, 'I'm sure you have thought of the money and also the fact that you will need to obtain markets for your lace products?'

'Thank you Mary, for the encouragement, and, yes, David, I have thought of marketing the lace. We are so fortunate in having merchants in the family, and of course the involvement of many of our friends in that trade, some of whom I have already approached. The Coppingers and Moylans have already helped in the employment of some of my boys, who have become proficient sailmakers. Do you remember my telling you about Paddy Dillon, who excelled in casting accounts? Mr Gould, who obtained a position for him, told me he is doing extremely well and that he has great hopes for him, and there are quite a few others I could mention. I think that by giving girls instruction in lacemaking, I could give them a similar opportunity to raise their position in life.'

'You can always count on our support, Nano, although at the moment obtaining access to our finances is somewhat difficult,' David told her. 'I think I should alert you that there are political rumblings which make me feel uneasy. One never knows what will happen. Do be careful,' David warned.

'Of course,' Nano smiled at him reassuringly. Inwardly she was thinking, dear cautious David. All my life I have been warned to be careful, and I have been, but I won't let my work, God's work, be stifled because of fear. It wasn't long before Nano was writing to Frances:

My dear Frances,
I can't tell you how much I still miss you and Joseph. You will both be pleased that my girls are becoming proficient lacemakers. Their pride in their work would bring tears to your eyes, Frances. Mr and Mrs Gould, the Coppingers and others are going to help with the distribution of the lace. I have a dream that lacemaking will become a home industry which will change women's lives dramatically. It is already giving my girls independence, and changing their perception of themselves. I notice there are fewer reported crimes against young women; this is because so many are in our classes until late, after which they walk home together, and are, therefore, not such easy targets. Their dress and behaviour have also improved.

I have also been admitting the children of prostitutes into my schools, with the result that I have recently been mocked by a certain group in the city, who accuse me of running houses of prostitution. Some have even followed me in the streets shouting abuse. I am telling you this in case you hear it from someone else and are worried about me. Although it is all very unpleasant and sometimes frightening, you need not fear for me. After all, this is God's work so I'm sure I will be protected, and I have many friends. It is a consolation that my schools are doing so well and the news of the good work is spreading rapidly.

I am pleased to hear that you and Joseph have made some wonderful new friends, while not forgetting your old ones. I hope you will visit soon.

Your affectionate sister,

Nano

Nano sat on her stool surrounded by the children whom she was preparing for first confession. She smiled at each one, her heart full of love for them. How God must love them, she thought. Her smile changed to a look of concern. There were two spaces.

'Where are Tommy and Lizzie Riley?' Nano asked.

'In gaol,' all the little voices chirped.

Nano was momentarily shocked into silence. These two were amongst her best students – always neat, clean, well-behaved little children whose parents worked hard in the meat markets. What could they have done? Before she could ask anything else, their little friend, Nancy, spoke up, 'They're all in gaol. All the family. We saw them carted off this morning, didn't we?'

Many of the children nodded solemnly.

Nano looked around the class and asked, 'Do you know why they were taken to gaol?'

'Yes, Miss Nagle,' answered Nancy 'My dada said Mr Riley hasn't been able to pay his rent, because the baby has been sick for so long and there aren't many cattle to sell this year. The owner of the house sent ... what's he called?' she appealed to the others.

'The bailiff,' answered one.

'Yes,' Nancy continued, 'the bailiff to take them to gaol until they pay all the money they own. That's why my dada is always worried about finding work. I heard him telling my mam that the same could happen to us if he couldn't find work. My mam said she was worried about the sick baby in gaol, too.'

Nano sighed but was careful to hide her distress from the children.

'Can you do anything for them, Miss Nagle?' pleaded Nancy. 'We're all so sad.'

The other children nodded in agreement, their large eyes fixed with hope.

'I'll see what I can do, children. Now let us begin our lessons. We will all pray for the Riley family and all the others in prison. But we always have to do something as well as pray, don't we?'

'I think all the men who threw the Rileys into gaol are terrible, and I'd like to—' Peter began vehemently, but was interrupted gently by Nano.

'You know I think it would be better if we closed our eyes, said a little prayer and thought of a kind deed we could do today, don't you?' she suggested.

There was a chorus of yeses while the children bent their heads to spend a few seconds in prayer and thought about a kindness they could do that day.

As for Nano, her prayers and thoughts for those imprisoned extended far beyond the classroom. Each day she passed the Cork City Gaol built over the Old Gate in the northern part of the city, or a similar one at the southern end of the city. The fate of the Riley family roused her interest in what was happening in these run-down, ominous-looking buildings. She had been aware that those awaiting trial, execution or transportation were sent there. There were so many times that she had consoled a grieving, abandoned family whose sole breadwinner was awaiting his fate within those dark, forbidding walls. Now she was made aware of entire families who were thrown into prison if they fell into debt. On her walks to her schools she had seen shopfronts boarded up, and had thought the families had moved. Now she discovered how many had fallen into debt, sometimes because of accidents, illness, or financial loss, and had been incarcerated as a result.

She asked one of her friends who knew the Rileys, 'What happens to the families in gaol? Are they ever released?'

'Nano, I'm sorry to say there are over fifty debtor families in the North Gate Gaol alone. Times are so difficult at the present, as there is very little work, and less money. In the gaol the family has to pay for everything: food, clothing, water, medicine if they can obtain it, bedding, and warmth – they are freezing places. Because they have no money they have to earn their keep by doing menial tasks, or rely on their friends or relatives to assist them. The gaols are dreadful places, Nano. People are thrown in together – the well, the sick, the good and bad, and often the gaolers are the worst of all. Keep away from them. I know you visit unsafe and unhealthy places, but please don't go the gaols, Nano.'

It proved too much of a challenge for Nano. I must see the Rileys, she thought. With her basket of food, ointments and bandages, and a purse of sovereigns, Nano, accompanied by her devoted Ellen, began her visits to the gaol. Although her years of experience in the most notorious sections of Cork had prepared her for the sordidness and depravity which existed in the gaol, she would never become accustomed to those who leered at her from the corners, or those who were habitually malevolent. Over time, with Nano's generosity, the Rileys and others obtained their freedom to begin their lives again. Nano never forgot the debtors who, through misfortune, found themselves in prison, and in her will she left money for their relief.

The years of unremitting service of others were beginning to take their toll on Nano's strength and health. Undeterred by how she felt, Nano continued her daily walk to all the schools, and twice a year she reserved to herself the instruction of children for sacramental confession. Although she said she felt unworthy to do this, it was something she delighted in. She kept a strict but kindly eye on the teachers she trained and employed to teach the non-religious subjects, and if disappointed in their intentions, or dedication to work, sadly dismissed them. The winter seasons were more difficult for her because it was then that her persistent cough became more troublesome and she would cough blood. Afraid that her family, friends or devoted teachers would prevent her walking to her schools, she managed to keep her health problems a secret. Nothing prevented her from dreaming of more solutions to the problems she saw resulting from the injustices existing in her world.

On occasions, she would receive visits from family members who asked about her works. Mary, Pierce, his son Patrick, and their own children Pierce, Margaret, Sarah, Teresa and James were infrequent but most welcome visitors. Nano was particularly enthralled with Elizabeth and Robert's growing family, Robert, Marion and Mary, and later Honoria (named after Nano), Frances and Margaret. On one such visit, Nano explained to Elizabeth her interest in the elderly poor.

'I am becoming really concerned about the numbers of poor who are abandoned. I was so troubled about what was happening to the children that I failed to notice the elderly women and men who die alone and uncared for in so many attics, and even on our streets. Some of the Protestant ones are cared for in the workhouses, which can contain between 400 to 800 people. I visit the North Infirmary which opened after that dreadful summer of 1740, when I believe that the streets were littered with those who died of starvation or fevers. I think it was about nine years later that the Cork Workhouse and Foundling Hospital were built, and it is overflowing too.'

'Who supports them? Are the people properly cared for?' queried an interested Elizabeth.

'They depend on donations, which makes their existence precarious. Sometimes the food is meagre and often atrocious. The beds are so close together it is difficult to walk between them, and usually they are occupied by a couple of people, most of whom are little more than skeletons. I find it so difficult when I see despair in their eyes. There is little that can be done to alleviate the pain of those suffering from illness or old age because of the lack of funds. Usually, all I can do is pray, and sit beside them. It must be so terrible to suffer and die alone, so I try to do all I can to let them know they are not alone and forgotten, and that there is someone who cares about them.'

'You said they were for Protestants – so what happens to the Catholics?' asked Elizabeth.

'That's what really worries me,' Nano replied. 'I don't like to talk about it, or even think of it,' she continued, 'But since you asked, I'll tell you. When I am going to the church early each morning I see the carts going around the lanes, along the canals and down the streets, gathering the bodies of those homeless who have died during the night.'

She was interrupted by a horrified gasp from Elizabeth. 'What do they do with the bodies?'

'That's what I wondered too, so one morning I asked a cart driver. He told me they take them to a section of the cemetery reserved for paupers, where they just dump the bodies into a massive pit. No one asks who they are. No one even says a prayer, unless the cart driver mutters a few words.'

There was a long silence while the two sisters reflected on the tragedy of those forgotten lives.

'Nano, I feel desperately sad, but what can we do? You are already doing so much. I really don't think we can do anything about the hundreds, perhaps thousands, who die in such a way. It's such a massive problem, because it no doubt occurs in all our cities. We'll have to pray that the law changes and we can restore our industries so that people can obtain employment. At least your schools are giving people skills.'

'I suppose you are right, Elizabeth. Now tell me about the children.'

Nano did, however, do much more than pray that the laws would change or that someone would come to the rescue of the elderly. She thought about how her work in the schools had spread from one little, hidden cottage and how it was transforming so many lives. If all this has happened from one set of actions, why can't something similar happen from others? I could build one small home for elderly destitute women. If that is successful I will then build one for men, and I'd really like to build something for poor prostitutes, whose desperate, violent lives touch my heart. She continued to confide all these thoughts to God as a plan evolved in her mind. Prayer, thought and careful, prudent planning became the order of the day.

Added to the worry about suitable teachers and avoiding trouble with the authorities was the fact that on occasions, Nano was unable to access finance to pay her teachers. Ultimately, she didn't manage to maintain her many works, or to achieve her dream of building the home for the elderly poor. Until she could augment her finances, all plans to assist the aged who had been abandoned would have to wait. Although her fortune was large, most of it consisted of investments, which the legal implications of the Penal Laws and the fluctuations of the market made difficult to avail of readily. It's so frustrating, Nano thought, that I so often have little ready money here in Ireland, when there is so much in my investments sitting in French banks. I shouldn't complain, because I am fortunate that both Papa and Uncle Joseph invested so wisely. However, if only we were friendlier with France, or weren't restricted by the Penal Laws, I wouldn't have these difficulties. Well, it's no use complaining; I'll have to think of alternatives. She mentioned one of her solutions to this problem in a letter to Joseph and Frances:

My dear brother and sister,
My thoughts and prayers are with you daily. In prior letters I have not spoken of my financial worries, as you perhaps suffer in the same way. My schools are my priority so I had to think of a way in which to sustain them until my money became available. I agonised over my solution, which was to beg. For days I thought I could not do it, but, eventually, when no other alternative presented itself, I set off. Yes, I did beg! I must admit I was trembling with fear, and spent sleepless nights at the prospect, but the thought of the kind-hearted shopkeepers and traders was a help. It makes my heart glad when they share the little they have. You will smile when I tell you of an amusing incident which resulted from my begging.

Early one morning I went to Driscoll's shop. Mr Driscoll has always been most generous, but I was there so early the shutters were still closed. I didn't have long to wait before the young lad employed there opened the shutters and, seeing me standing outside, brusquely asked what I was doing. With a smile I told him I wished to see Mr Driscoll. In a rather rude voice he demanded why, whereupon I informed him that Mr Driscoll always gave me a generous donation. To my amazement he snorted disdainfully, 'What! A beggar? We see more than enough of them around here. Now, get out!'

I didn't want to humiliate him by saying who I was, and as I thought he wouldn't dare pick me up to throw me out, I sat down on a coil of rope and said I would wait for Mr Driscoll, even if I had to wait all day. He muttered a curse and took himself off to arrange some goods, although he kept an eye on me, perhaps suspecting I would steal something. Fortunately, not long after, I heard Mr Driscoll's arrival. The young man rushed over to tell him of my presence. To my amusement I heard him say, 'Mr Driscoll, sir, there's a very shabby, old lady in there, all dressed in black. She's one of those lazy, disreputable beggars. She refused to go, and demanded to see you, sir. I tried, but couldn't get rid of her, but I kept an eye on her. I hope she's not harmful, sir.'

'Thank you, Dan,' Mr Driscoll replied as he parted the curtain between the workroom and the shop.

Poor Mr Driscoll looked shocked and humiliated when he saw me. With outstretched hands he welcomed me, apologising profusely. Although I at first refused the cup of tea and scone he offered me, he was so mortified that I left after a substantial breakfast and with a sizable donation. I would have loved to hear what he said to his young employee, but whatever it was, I pray it changed his attitude to the poor.

I have found a very good, sheltered corner on Shandon Street where I can sit to beg when I am desperate for money. Never fear, Joseph, people are coming to know me, so I am quite safe, and it is amazing how generous people are, especially the less well-to-do.

Around that time, the Nagle brothers lived in fear of a backlash from the violence of roving bands of disgruntled men who burnt, looted and murdered tax collectors, landlords and those who occupied lands appropriated from Catholics. Because of the white shirts they wore over their clothes they became known as Whiteboys. Their anger and vengeance spread over to the mistreatment of animals as they rampaged through the country, slaughtering cattle, pigs, sheep, dogs and poultry. The English feared that the French would support the Whiteboys with an invasion, while the Catholics feared a more severe retaliation from the anti-Catholics. Amidst these uncertainties, the poor suffered more than ever. Nano read in the paper the report of a traveller who wrote that the 'poor reduced wretches have hardly the skin of a potato left them to subsist on'.

'I wish we could do more to help these poor people,' Nano complained to Joseph on one of his visits.

'You are certainly doing everything you can, Nano. There are some who publicly denounce the injustices. Cousin Edmund Burke is one of them. Another is Dean Jonathan Swift, the satirist who is always putting pen to paper. Did you read his proposals in the paper last week?'

Nano laughed. 'Yes I did. His suggestions are sometimes ludicrous. This time he certainly captured people's attention when he suggested the best way to save the starving children is to eat them! There was such outrage, as of course he intended.'

'Nano, I think you should be especially careful these days.' Joseph warned. 'Mr Gould told me that the government fears a Catholic uprising because of all this activity from the Whiteboys.'

'Joseph, don't worry. You know how careful I am,' Nano assured him.

Soon after, David arrived with a worried frown on his face. 'I can't stay long as I have a business appointment, but I heard that Andrew Franklin, the Mayor, has ordered Colonel

Molesworth, commander of the city garrison, to mount a military guard in the area around Saint Finbarr's near your schools because there are rumours of a popish plot being hatched in this area. I also heard that Protestants have been told to wear swords and have firearms in their homes as a protection. You really are in danger, Nano.'

'Thank you, David, for the warning. Rest assured I will take every care. I certainly don't wish to place my children and the teachers in any danger,' Nano promised.

Nano personally thought that her schools would be safe, not only because it was God's work, but because of her astute planning and the great benefits she was rendering the city. If her schools were destroyed or closed the crime rate would rise, which would mean that the wealthy would live in fear for their property, the number of vagrants would increase, and the problems of the Cork City Council would multiply. She did, however, confer with her teachers, as their lives were also in danger. They agreed with Nano that they continue as they had always done. It was a wise move, because Colonel Molesworth, not agreeing with the order, questioned the Mayor's authority in this matter. In the ensuing quarrel, the fear of a plot disappeared.

Although Nano knew of her brothers' disquiet over the dangerous times, she was crestfallen in 1762 when Joseph and Frances, followed by David and Mary, visited her with the news that they were moving to Bath, England, where there was a settlement of Irish who had fled the unrest.

'Won't you come with us, Nano?' pleaded Joseph, 'You know how unsafe it is becoming again here, and now we don't have Uncle Joseph to defend us. You will be so alone. With David and me in England, and Mary and Elizabeth so far away, who will be near to support you? We'll be so worried about you, won't we Frances?'

'Indeed we will. I thought we were a long way away when we moved to Holyhill, but now we won't even be in the country. Please do come, Nano.'

Nano smiled at these two beloved people. 'I do appreciate your kindness and always will; but you both know that I cannot leave my schools, or indeed any of my poor people. I would never be at peace if I abandoned them for my own safety and pleasure. I hear that Bath is a beautiful place and we have relatives nearby, and I do promise that I will visit when I am able.'

With these assurances Joseph and Frances had to be satisfied. When they sailed from Cork harbour they both stayed on deck until they could no longer see the small, lonely figure waving from the wharf. Fortunately, they were unable to see the tears that escaped to silently course down Nano's tired face.

Soon after her arrival home, she received a letter from Teresa Mulally telling of her parents' death. Feeling bereft herself, Nano immediately wrote comforting words to her young friend, who was planning to devote her life to improving the situation of the disadvantaged children who wandered the streets near her in Dublin. She concluded her letter by offering any help she could.

CHAPTER EIGHT

The winter was particularly cold. As Nano struggled against the bitterly cold wind, which whipped her cloak about her frail frame, and seemed to seek out her bones and to take away her breath, she reflected on how tired she felt. I must think about the future of my schools, she thought, and about all those I visit. I haven't done anything about the abandoned elderly people yet, either. So many people tell me I work too hard, and I'm realising I won't be able to carry on this work much longer. As was her practice, she voiced her concerns through her conversations with God, and as usual God did not fail her. Her conclusions reached, she decided to confide them to the curate, Father Francis Moylan. Francis had returned from France, where he, like the Nagle family, had gone for education. After finishing school, he had entered a seminary; now, with his uncle, the Jesuit, Father Doran, he was back in Cork. Both were becoming noted for their empathy with the poor of the city. Both, too, were great admirers of Nano's works. Father Doran's Jesuit friend, Father Mulcaile, went to Dublin, where he met a parishioner named Teresa Mulally. Like his two friends in Cork and Teresa, he was disturbed by the conditions of the poor, especially the children. Teresa wrote to Nano of her good fortune in having the support of 'this good priest'.

After Mass one morning, Nano approached Father Moylan asking if he could spare her some time that day.

'Yes, of course, Nano. Perhaps we could meet later in the day when you have finished your work in the schools. Would that be satisfactory?' he asked.

'Father, that would be splendid. Perhaps you would like to come to supper?'

Father Moylan accepted the invitation with alacrity. That evening he listened wide-eyed to Nano's plans for the continuation of her works.

'Nano, that's a daring idea,' he said when Nano had finished describing how she planned to bring a religious congregation to Cork to carry her work into the future.

'Daring!' laughed Nano. 'How can you say I am daring when you and your uncle are so daring in coming back to Cork? You were successful in Paris, and although your uncle, being a Jesuit, was expelled from France, he could have gone to some safer place. I hear, too, that Father Mulcaile is doing wonderful work in Dublin.'

Francis Moylan merely smiled, then continued, 'I don't know if your plan will succeed. Didn't I hear that the Bishop of Galway has made two attempts to bring religious sisters to his diocese, both of which failed. If a bishop was not successful, I doubt if you can be. There is also the fact that it is illegal to have a religious house in Ireland. Convents have been destroyed and religious dispersed, and in some cases actually killed. I know there are some who live in disguise and work secretly, but you are planning to actually build a convent and bring a congregation here.'

'All you say is true,' Nano agreed, 'But Catholic schools are forbidden, too, and many Catholic teachers have been hunted down, executed or transported, yet I have a system of schools and wonderful teachers. I have always done everything I can to protect them, and so far we have been very successful.'

'Nano, you really are incorrigible, and I wonder what your brothers will say about this latest plan of yours. I do admire your courage, prudence and astuteness. Your father and uncle were the same. Of course I will support you in any way I can. Would you like to tell my uncle of your plans, as he is such a wise and experienced man?'

'I was hoping you would support me, Father, and I will speak with your uncle, who is so dedicated to the poor of Cork.'

Father Doran, on account of his respect for Nano and her works, pledged his support.

More confident now that she had the support of the two curates, Nano approached Bishop Butler, the Bishop of Cork, with her plans. After all, we are related, she thought, and he is quite friendly with the Protestant Bishop, which is a great advantage. As she had hoped, Bishop Butler listened patiently and with interest to Nano's proposal to bring a religious congregation to Cork. The Bishop secretly admired the courage and faith of this woman who was having such an impact on the city. When she had finished speaking, he asked pertinent questions about where she would build, how she would finance her venture, where she would find suitable religious, and what she would expect of them. Nano had an answer for each question, although she was not quite sure which congregation to approach. Satisfied that Nano was well prepared, the Bishop gave his consent, but advised her to seek permission from the Protestant authorities. Privately he had his doubts about the success of the project.

'You know, Nano, the law requires that we obtain permission to exercise as priests, to set up chapels, celebrate Mass or do anything that helps spread our faith. We are not even permitted to build churches, although we may build chapels.'

'Thank you, My Lord,' Nano smilingly replied, 'but I believe every child has the right to a Catholic education and it is an injustice to deny that right, so to ask permission, I believe, is condoning that injustice.'

To this the Bishop had no answer, and for some time after she left he sat reflecting on the bravery of this little woman. If I hadn't asked permission, been registered, and given surety I wouldn't move from this diocese, and paid my fees to allow me to practise as a priest, I would not be here, he rationalised. Anyway, I have given up so much to minister to the people, even if many of my friends are wealthy. My friendship with that fine fellow the Bishop has been of great benefit to others as well as to me.

The more Nano thought and prayed about her idea, the more convinced she became that this was the solution to make sure her works would continue. She also thought deeply about what type of religious she would need, and gradually a picture emerged in her mind. To the two priests she described what she envisaged.

'I need a religious congregation which will devote itself to the poor in both the schools and the streets, but above all, in the schools. They must have a reputation as excellent teachers, and be women of prayer. Of course, they would need to be aware of the political situation in Ireland, but not be deterred by that.'

Father Moylan smiled. 'Nano, as usual you have clear ideas about what you want, and are determined to achieve your goals. I do, however, wonder if you will find any order brave enough to come to Cork in these troubled and dangerous times.'

Father Doran, who had been listening attentively, made a suggestion. 'Nano, have you thought of the Ursulines? We know they have a remarkable reputation as teachers, and they are also contemplatives. Both of you would know them from your years in France. Didn't your cousin, Margaret Butler, enter the Ursulines in St Denis?'

'Yes,' answered Nano. 'She is to receive the habit in December.'

'The Ursulines sound like a good idea,' Father Moylan agreed. 'Nano, as a member of a mercantile family, you would have heard of the Ursuline missionary work, especially in New Orleans, where they have a flourishing and most successful school.'

'Yes, I do know of that foundation, which would have presented such difficulties. I also heard of that wonderful woman, Marie de l'Incarnation, who led a band of Ursuline Sisters to Canada to teach the Hurons, the Iroquois and the Algonquin. What could be braver than that?'

Father Moylan responded, 'Many think of the Ursulines only as an enclosed order of great teachers of the more wealthy.'

At this Father Doran nodded in agreement.

'But', continued Father Moylan, 'seeing that they have educated Irish girls for so many decades, and have two successful missions, maybe they will consent to come to Ireland.'

Nano hesitated. 'Let me think about it,' she said. 'The spirituality of the nuns I wish to have is very important to me. Jansenism is rife in parts of France, as you are aware, so I wouldn't want that influence. I believe that its emphasis on moral austerity, the evil of the human body and human desires, and its notion that salvation is reserved for a select few, is an injustice to God's love and mercy. Some orders also spend so much time in prayer that I wonder if they have time for the service of others. I would require a balance of prayer and service.'

'Quite right,' agreed Father Doran. 'Nano, take all the time you need before making a decision. When would you like to meet with us again?'

Nano reflected for a moment. 'Could I let you know when I have come to a decision?'

'Of course, Nano,' they said in unison.

The more Nano prayed and thought about the conversation, the more sure she became that the Ursulines would be a good choice. She discovered that, although they were committed to the education of the well-to-do, a clause in their constitutions required that they also provide schools for the poor. Nano found, moreover, that she had an affinity with the Ursuline spirituality. Their rule was highly spiritual and they were primarily women of contemplative prayer. There was another factor which influenced her, namely, their practice of providing catechetical instruction on holidays to domestics and women from the poorer sections of society. Their education was focused on females, and the organisation of their monastic life was modified to allow them to carry on their ministry. Yes, she thought. To invite the Ursulines seems an answer to my dilemma.

When the two priests came to hear Nano's decision, they were not surprised.

'We must keep in mind that if you bring a group of religious women to Ireland, especially from France, England's enemy at the moment, a great deal of trouble could occur,' Father Doran warned.

'True,' agreed his nephew.

'Ever since I returned from the convent and began my schools, I have been told of the dangers, which I know are real,' Nano replied, 'I live with them everyday and have never taken them lightly, especially when they involve so many people, whom I would not put in danger. I firmly believe this is God's work, so I place my trust in him and anyone he sends to help.'

'I agree with you, Nano. I am actually going to France later this year – would you like me to visit the Ursulines in the Rue St Jacques?'

'It seems fortuitous that you are going to France; I think we should make use of this opportunity,' Nano said. Turning to Father Doran, she added, 'I know you would love to go, Father, but since you Jesuits have been expelled from France it would be foolhardy. I will be happy to have your support here in Cork.'

In the summer of 1767, Father Moylan approached the Ursulines at the Rue St Jacques about the possibility of an establishment in Cork. Mother Elizabeth Jeanne Berjonneau de St Cyprien politely answered that she would discuss the matter with the twenty-five sisters who lived there. However, none of the sisters dared to venture to Ireland, where the statutes, if adhered to, would mean death or deportation.

'Why go there when we have so many demands on us here?' they asked.

Father Moylan's hopes were dashed, but he did not give up. 'I understand, Mother Elizabeth Jeanne, how you all feel about this. I wonder if you would train any Irish girls we find who would dedicate themselves as Ursulines in Cork? Miss Nagle has promised to pay all the expenses which would be involved. Although she sometimes has difficulty in obtaining finances in Ireland, she has no problems here in France.'

After discussions with the Novice Mistress, Mother Marie Thérèse Petit de Saint Joseph, Mother Elizabeth Jeanne agreed to accept and train in their novitiate any candidates for the Irish mission; however, it would have to be an independent foundation, as Paris would not accept any responsibility for it. They did not voice their concerns, but they had no doubts that the foundation would be a failure. A relieved Father Moylan wrote the good news to Nano:

Dear Miss Nagle,

At last I have the pleasure of informing you that, although the sisters at Rue St Jacques will not send sisters to Cork, they have agreed to accept and train any volunteers we may get. As you instructed, I have assured them that you will pay all the expenses involved. Now we need to find young ladies who wish to join your venture. I will do my best to find any among the Irish group who reside in Paris. You, with all your contacts, may know some in Ireland who, like yourself, are courageous and dedicated.

Remember me before the Lord,
Francis Moylan

Nano shared the good news with her friend, Teresa Mulally, who was quick to reply:

Dear Miss Nagle,
How delighted I was to hear of your arrangements with the Parisian Ursulines. Ever since, I have been thinking of anyone who might be suitable, and also willing, to join your Ursulines. I'm sure you have heard of the Fitzsimons family who support my work with the children here. Mr Thomas Fitzsimons is a merchant who lives nearby in Saint Michan's Parish. He and his wife, Mary, have a daughter, Eleanor, who is well educated, devout, a potential leader and, like the rest of her family, very devoted to the poor here in the parish. I heard she is now in Paris preparing to enter the Sisters of the Visitation. I wonder if Father Moylan, who is so charming and can be very persuasive, could influence her to change her mind to join your group?

You know I decided to open a small school for orphans and deprived children. Father Mulcaile assisted me in finding a house. I rented the back room of an old three-storeyed building in Mary's Lane, near the chapel. We are drafting a letter of appeal for funds from the wealthy of the parish. I am adopting your ideas in my classes and hope you will aid me further and keep me in your prayers.

Your affectionate friend,
Teresa Mulally

Nano acted immediately on Teresa's suggestion, contacting Father Moylan who, already mixing with the Irish group in Paris, had heard that some of the young Irish women were planning to join French convents. He lost no time in making contact with them. His personal experience with the poor in both Paris and Cork and his deep compassion for them, especially the children, added significance to his plea. As such, he provoked a response in Eleanor Fitzsimons, who abandoned her idea of joining the Sisters of the Visitation and instead agreed to join what was to become known as the Irish Ursulines.

Nano made her decisions with her usual attention to detail. She would go to the Ursuline convent at St Denis, where her cousin was, to have first-hand experience and knowledge of how the Ursulines lived. While there, she would also improve her meagre knowledge of French, most of which she had forgotten. She believed a better knowledge to be essential if she was to communicate with the French Sisters. She remained there for seven months, after which she felt confident that she knew a sufficient amount about the Ursuline way of life and their rules. She also felt more comfortable with the French language if ever she needed it. To be thoroughly prepared, she persuaded her cousin Margaret, who had been professed on 19 December 1765 and was now Sister Francis, to accompany her back to Cork where she could give further advice and support. After Sister Francis obtained permission from the Archbishop of Paris, she, dressed in secular clothes for the sake of safety, accompanied Nano to Cork on 28 August 1767.

It was a cold, snowy day in November 1767 when Father Moylan accompanied Eleanor Fitzsimons to the Ursuline convent in the Rue St Jacques as the first postulant for the Cork foundation. Although he was still disappointed at the failure of their original plan to bring the French Ursulines, Nano's optimism boosted his own.

'We have begun,' Nano rejoiced. 'Surely we can encourage some other Irish girls from Cork or nearby to join Eleanor.'

Buoyed by this hope, Nano reflected on possible candidates from the Cork mercantile families with whom she was familiar, and who were noted for their loyalty to their faith. Her thoughts came to rest on one of her cousins, Margaret Nagle, the daughter of her cousin David and his wife Mary Denny, who lived in what was known as The Cathedral Parish in North Cork. There was no hesitation on Margaret's part, but she met with forceful opposition from her parents, who were afraid of the consequences if their daughter was a religious.

'You know very well, Margaret, what has happened to other religious in Ireland. Think of the Poor Clares, the Dominicans and the Carmelites. Do you want to spend your life in hiding and in fear?' her father asked.

'Father, I do know the dangers, but I also know that is what God wants me to do. I am proud of what our family in the past has suffered to keep their faith, and I am no less faithful. I know, too, how prudent Nano is. Papa, look at how successful she has been with her schools, and how she has protected her teachers. I'm sure I will be safe. If Eleanor is brave enough, so am I.'

Eventually, Mary wore down the fear and resistance of her parents. Father Doran, meanwhile, was not idle. It seemed natural that he would turn to the wealthy, well-educated families who had maintained their faith through the turbulence of the Penal years. He approached Elizabeth Coppinger, a member of the well-connected Coppinger family who, like the Nagles, had suffered under the Penal Laws. Some of their members had gone into exile in France, and others had settled in America. Unlike the Nagles, the Coppingers were happy about their daughter's choice, but insisted that she obtain permission from her great-aunt, Dame Mary Butler. Although fearful for her grand-niece, Dame Mary did give her consent.

Everything proceeded slowly, with many frustrations for Nano and her supporters. In 1768 it seemed as though there would be five young women to begin the novitiate, but gradually, because of fear, the numbers dwindled. One of the most promising had been a Miss Shea.

'My dear, your mother and I are so pleased about your desire, but we do not think it wise. As well as the dangers you would face, we really believe that the venture will not be a success; everything points to a failure. We are unable to give our approval,' Mr Shea told his daughter.

Upon hearing this, Father Moylan did his best to allay the family's fears. After a few unsuccessful attempts, Father Moylan took his concerns to Nano.

'Father, I don't think we should press Mr Shea to give permission. We must remember that she is his darling daughter, and he does not wish her to go to France, which is understandable. She would be there for several years, a separation which is too much for them at this time. Surely, Mr Shea's faith will prevail, and, this, together with your encouraging words, will eventually lead him to give his consent.'

Another who expressed interest was Mary Moylan, half-sister to Father Moylan. Nano's faith in Father Moylan's powers of persuasion was in vain, however, for neither Mary Moylan nor Miss Shea entered for the Cork mission. Eleanor Fitzsimons remained alone for nearly two years, a beacon of hope amidst all the disappointments, and the only woman sustaining Nano's dream of a religious foundation in Cork. In that time letters frequently passed between the two women who had never met, but between whom an enduring belief and affection was being built. Nano's letters of encouragement nourished Eleanor's commitment, while Eleanor's informative and faithful accounts cemented Nano's trust in her first candidate.

In the summer of 1769, Elizabeth Coppinger and Margaret Nagle bid farewell to their still-fearful families and set sail for France, where they intended to spend a few days in Paris with Mary Kavanagh, a cousin of Elizabeth's, before entering at the Rue St Jacques. Mary had arrived earlier with the intention of joining a French religious community. An enthusiastic Elizabeth and Margaret soon persuaded Mary to change her mind and to join them. Nano's hopes rose when she received the news, which she shared at once with the two priests. She wrote to the patient Eleanor on 17 July 1769:

> I cannot express how much I suffered on your account; you must have been very uneasy when you did not hear of the arrival of the young ladies we had expected to join you ... I have met Miss Coppinger but do not really know her, but I do rely on Father Doran's opinion, and he is very impressed with her. I am sorry she has not seen the schools, because, unless one is an eye-witness one cannot have an idea of what is accomplished ...
>
> I can assure you my schools are beginning to be of service to a great many parts of the world ... If I could be of service in saving souls in any part of the globe I would willingly do all in my powers to do so ... Father Moylan wishes to be remembered to you.

Eleanor's face was a picture of happiness on 5 September 1769 when she was joined in the novitiate by Elizabeth Coppinger and Mary Nagle. Elizabeth gave her another piece of good news: 'My cousin, Mary Kavanagh, is anxious to join us so has returned to Ireland to speak about her vocation with her parents, who, I am confident, will agree to allow her to come. They'll no doubt speak to Aunt Butler, but I think she will be quite pleased, as she was about me.'

The three waited anxiously for favourable news from the Kavanaghs, and were not disappointed when a letter arrived sometime later telling them that Mary would enter within the year. Their joy was increased when the letter also added that Mary's sister, Nano, also wished to join them.

Nano was overjoyed when a Miss Lawless, a daughter of a master cooper who lived in Ryrles Quay, Cork, expressed a wish to go to Paris as a postulant for the Irish foundation. Mr Lawless, however, refused permission.

'We couldn't think of allowing you to go to France to enter a convent. We all know of the terrible political unrest; what we don't know is how far it will spread, and how violent it will be now that the Jesuits have already been expelled. I suspect all convents will be closed. No, we could never give permission for such folly,' he assured his daughter, and nothing moved him from this decision. Seeing the sadness on his daughter's face, he relented by suggesting that she go to Liege in Flanders.

'Papa,' she argued, 'Father Austin thinks I'll be safe. Fathers Doran and Moylan agree with him, and, remember they have recently returned from France. I really wish to go to the Rue St Jacques where the other girls are.'

Her father vigorously questioned Father Austin, who admitted that he was worried about the success of Nano's plan. On hearing this, Mr Lawless's opposition grew. He offered his daughter many enticements, including a dowry of £2,000 to marry, as she had no dearth of suitors. At first she resisted the offers and arranged to meet Nano to discuss the matter with her. However, at the last moment her courage failed, and she accepted her father's proposal. On receiving the news, Nano was deeply saddened.

Although suffering another blow to her dreams, Nano did not forget what Eleanor must be enduring herself.

'We must believe the Almighty permits everything for the best. You'll see that with his assistance everything will be well,' she wrote to Eleanor. In her little room, with the flickering light of her candle casting dancing shadows against the paper, she continued, 'I hope your courage and faith will bring you through all crosses and bring about a happy conclusion to this foundation.'

Putting down her pen, Nano thought of Eleanor, alone for so long, and now so far away while having to make important decisions which could affect the growth of the Irish foundation. Nano knew only too well how that felt. I must assure her of my confidence in her and that, whatever decisions she makes, she has my full support. She took up her pen to finish the letter, telling Eleanor to spare no expense for anything she thought essential for the success of their venture, adding that they were all happy to have a person of good sense such as herself to guide them. 'I can with truth say you are under God, the chief support of this good work which I am sure will prosper,' she assured her before signing off, 'I am, my dear Miss Fitzsimons, your most affectionate friend, Nano Nagle.'

With the hope that her letter of appreciation and trust would show Eleanor affectionate support, Nano sealed it in preparation for the following day's post.

In 1768, as part of her plan to bring a religious congregation to Cork, Nano needed to purchase an area of land on which to build a suitable convent. After some thought, she decided to reclaim some land once owned by Uncle Joseph. For some time Nano had been feeling that Sister Francis had not been happy. On 9 August, Nano was saddened but not surprised when Sister Francis told her that she could no longer remain in Cork. She felt too isolated from her community and had doubts about the success of Nano's plan. Nano wondered how many more setbacks she would have to endure. She had hoped that her cousin would remain to help the Irish Ursulines settle in.

On 23 December 1768, Nano signed an indenture leasing land in South Cork from Isabella Harper, the widow of John Harper. On this site she began the building of her Ursuline convent. Now that her plans were underway, she would visit her brothers in Bath to inform them of her decisions.

Calling Mary Fouhy and her other teachers together, she told them of her intended trip to Bath and prepared them to share some of her daily rounds. The evening before her departure, her band of loyal teachers gathered to pray with her and to wish her a successful and enjoyable time with her family.

'Miss Nagle, it's about time you went to see your family. We are so pleased you are going, although we will miss your listening ear and your encouraging words. You know we will do all in our power to carry out your wishes while you are away,' Mary assured her.

'Yes, indeed,' they all affirmed, although the younger ones felt some trepidation at the task ahead of them.

Settled on the boat, Nano had time to reflect on how she had really struggled to drag herself away from her children. I hope my new little teacher, Elizabeth, manages well. Of course she will, she chided herself. I make sure I choose only the best and train them well. Dear Mary will be a great support to her, as she has been to all my teachers. How blessed I have been! I've done my best, so now I'll leave everything to God and my teachers. With these thoughts, Nano settled back to enjoy the rest of the trip to Bath.

Joseph and Frances couldn't wait for her to arrive at their home at Number 7, the Paragon Buildings in Bath. When she alighted from the carriage Joseph's hug almost deprived her of breath; Frances's more gentle one also told of her longing for Nano's visit. There was barely a moment's silence in the hours which followed, until Frances said, 'Joseph, we are being so selfish. Poor Nano must be exhausted. We should all say goodnight. We can continue our conversation in the days to come.'

Nano did suddenly feel tired. When they all retired for the night, it didn't take her long to fall into a dreamless sleep in the large, soft feather bed surrounded by rich trinkets and tapestries. In the morning, when she was awakened by her old maid, Ellen, for a moment she wondered where she was. Was she dreaming? Had she stepped back into her youth? She then saw Ellen, her once fresh youthful face, now lined but still peaceful and kind. Both women smiled. No, she was here in Bath. This luxury was temporary and she would soon be back in her small, frugal house – but she had something important to do before she returned. She had no doubts about Joseph's and Frances's response, but was not so confident about David and Mary. They are much more cautious, she mused, and David is such a worrier.

Joseph and Frances listened in silence to Nano's proposal. They were apprehensive on account of the dangers, but knew well Nano's determination and her capacity and faith when dealing with difficult situations. Without hesitation, they promised all the support which would be needed. Nano then told them of her interview with the Bishop and his suggestion that she obtain permission to bring a religious order to Cork. Joseph snorted. 'Permission! Nano I think you are quite right to refuse such a notion. It's not right that we cannot have religious orders in Ireland. We are behind you on this, as we are with your schools, aren't we Frances?'

'Yes, indeed,' agreed Frances. 'We have every confidence in your prudence, and we have seen how you plan and organise your schools, so we're sure your establishment of a convent will be just as successful.'

Nano's meeting with David and Mary in their residence at 31 Milsom Street was a little more difficult, as it took extra time to convince them that this latest project was not fraught with too many difficulties. Nano was pleased to have Joseph's support when she told David of the Bishop's request. 'If the Bishop asked permission, I don't see why that is not good enough for you. What harm can it do?' David said.

Joseph didn't wait for Nano's reply. 'Permission could be refused, David, but I don't see that is the point; it's that we have to ask permission in the first place. It's absolutely wrong! I agree with Nano. No, Nano, don't ask permission! It's a reinforcing of the injustices.'

David opened his mouth to speak, but hesitated for a moment before replying, 'Of course, my dear. We are indeed proud of you, Nano, and you have our wholehearted support.'

'Have you decided where to build your convent?' asked Mary.

'Oh, yes, I meant to mention that I have bought a site.' Nano went on to describe the site and the beginning of the building construction.

Later, David explained his point of view to Mary. 'I really think she should ask permission. This is such a dangerous step. We know, however, that when Nano makes up her mind, arguments are futile.'

'Don't worry, David,' Mary comforted him. 'We also know how shrewd Nano is, and, as Uncle Joseph always proclaimed, she is an excellent businesswoman. Actually, she is very like Uncle Joseph in that respect. I believe she will be safe.'

Both families made sure that Nano enjoyed her visit to their beautiful adopted city. They organised visits to the Pump Room, which had been erected in 1706 and enlarged in 1751, and in which Joseph had shares which were quite lucrative. Joseph arranged sedan chairs to transport them to the splendid building. What a luxury, Nano thought. She chuckled inwardly as she thought of how incongruous it would be if she took a sedan chair in Cork. In the Pump Room they walked in the promenade and sat to listen to the Pump Room Band. As time ran out that day, the chairs were also organised to take them back the following day to the Roman Baths. There, Nano admired the Roman building expertise which had resulted in these extraordinary facilities. Fortunately they were not as busy as usual, so Nano was able to inspect them at leisure. Nano found the whole visit entertaining and enjoyable – but no joy compared with the time she spent with the family.

'You must come again, Nano. Frances and I are thinking of moving to The Circus, which is more central, and more comfortable,' Joseph told Nano the day before she left for Cork.

'It would please us so much if you could come to visit us there,' Frances added.

'Thank you both for everything. I have had a most enjoyable time, and do feel much rested,' Nano replied, without promising to return to Bath. Refreshed and happy with her brothers' support, she returned to her work in Cork, and her preparations for the Ursuline foundation there. One of her first visits was to her building site, where the workmen, some of whom had worked on her schools and were aware of her attention to detail, were meticulous in carrying out her wishes. They were also the recipients of her dedication to paying just wages and her interest in their working conditions, which resulted in their increased efforts to satisfy her requests and needs. Set back from the street as she had requested, the building was beginning to take shape as a large, imposing building, its progress impeded only by bad weather. Nano was pleased to see its development since her trip to Bath. She wrote to Eleanor Fitzsimons to say that it could be habitable by the winter.

Her visits to her schools were equally pleasing. In the past she had sadly had to dismiss teachers who were not satisfactory, but now she saw the impressive results of her teachers' devotion, dedication and care. She smiled with delight when her boys showed her some of their completed tasks. I am so pleased that Frances insisted I take boys, she thought. The girls proudly demonstrated their prowess in reading, writing, arithmetic and their knowledge of the catechism. The bigger girls showed their talents in lacemaking and sewing. Some were already earning money which in time would help support their families. A truly grateful Nano called her teachers together to express her thanks and appreciation for their transforming work.

Anxious to hear news from their friends in Bath, the Moylans invited Nano to dinner. 'We did consider moving too,' Mr Moylan informed Nano, 'But our son, Francis, as you know has returned from France, so we decided to stay. When we sent him to school in France we hoped he would join us in our shipping business. We are proud, of course, that he chose the priesthood, but do worry about him here.'

'Do tell us about your visit to Bath, Nano. I've heard there are quite a few Irish families there now, and that it is a well-known venue for those wishing to take the baths for their health,' Mrs Moylan prompted.

'I did hear there was a rumour that I went there to take the waters,' Nano smiled. 'But, as you are aware, I went to visit my family who are all in good health, and feel quite safe. They are becoming known there for their generosity to the less fortunate, as, of course, they were here. They sent their regards and were interested in all the news from home. Although they have settled into their new homes, they miss all their friends. I did enjoy my time with them, and I can assure you Bath is a beautiful and interesting little place. Both my brothers and their wives told me to make sure I passed on their invitations to you to visit them anytime.'

'Thank you, Nano. Your family has always been noted for its generosity,' Mr Moylan replied. 'I heard that some of your boys have obtained work with the builders of your convent, which, I observed, is progressing well, if slowly, although I did hear the plaster is drying quickly.'

'Yes,' Nano replied proudly. 'When I was there yesterday, John, the foreman, told me how pleased he was with the boys' reliability. He was very impressed with how meticulous they were in their measurements. I was so happy to see young Tommy Riley among the apprentices, because he was always one of our best students, and suffered that unfortunate incident of being cast into gaol with his family.'

'Nano, you are too modest,' Mr Moylan interrupted. 'We heard it was you who rescued that family and that you continue to rescue many others.'

'I think your schools are performing miracles. No wonder the city council turns a blind eye to your activities. The streets and businesses are so much safer. I must tell you that I heard from the Goulds that your girls' lace is a great success. Do you think they could make me a few lace caps for my girls?' Mrs Moylan asked.

'We'd be happy to do that,' Nano answered.

She turned to Mr Moylan. 'Now that my brothers are living in Bath I don't hear as much about the shipping trade, or how things are going for those Irish who have gone, or been sent, to the American colonies.'

Before he could reply Mrs Moylan spoke sadly, 'I can't explain how I feel when I think of all those poor Irish boys and girls who, in the past, have been sent as slaves to work in the sugar or tobacco plantations. There are, too, some still being sent because they break the Penal Laws, or are orphans, and others who are taken from the streets. I hear many there are deprived of an education, or even knowledge of their faith. Someone, I think it was Mrs Coppinger, told me that there were over 100,000 Irish sent as slaves to Jamaica and Barbados, and many have been sent elsewhere as well.'

'It's a pity you cannot set up a school there, Nano,' Mr Moylan said.

In the next few days Nano began to think of her discussion with the Moylans about the poor Irish in the Americas. She recalled conversations she had heard from other shipping families of the superstition and ignorance of the poor Irish in the colonies. It was injustice which had taken them away from their homeland, and it was injustice which kept them in ignorance and want.

Together with her thirst for justice, her love of God and people, there was her desire to bring about a better world. Hadn't she written to Eleanor claiming she would go anywhere in the world to be of assistance? I can't build a school there, but surely there is something I can do, she thought. During her visits to the boys' schools and the building site, she watched the enthusiasm and commitment of her boys and young men, and gradually the seed of an idea was planted in her mind.

This was when she most missed her family, in particular Joseph and Frances. With whom could she discuss the idea she was developing? She took it to her talks with God. I know, she thought, I could discuss it with my merchant friends who are familiar with the colonies, and whose assistance will be of value too. After speaking with God, it was to her teachers and the merchants that she revealed her unfolding plan.

'I'm going to need your support and assistance if this is to be successful,' she told the teachers in her boys' schools before she spoke to the merchants.

To the gathered teachers she explained what she had in mind. 'We have educated all our children to help others and to share their gifts. Some, we know, are skilful in helping other children to learn, and they take special pride in doing so. I think we could train our more skilled ones to go to the colonies, to educate in the faith those poor people who are longing for knowledge. We could begin in Jamaica, I suggest. There are past students who are already engaged in trade with Jamaica, so we could help them with their teaching skills. I'll make sure they are financially supported.'

Once their initial hesitation over finance was overcome, the teachers enthusiastically embraced the idea. Much discussion and planning followed. 'I'll purchase pictures and anything else the boys will need for their instruction,' Nano assured them.

'We'll pray for your success when you speak with some of your merchant friends, and in the meantime we will think of some boys who would be likely to respond to your invitation, Miss Nagle,' they declared.

Nano then approached some of the merchants, including the Moylans, who had supported her over the decades. Some, whose interests went beyond the profits accrued from trade, congratulated Nano, promising financial support and passages for the boys in their ships. Others expressed doubts about the success of the enterprise.

'Miss Nagle, don't you think you are being too optimistic? How do you know some won't use your money to set themselves up in the colony?'

Others derided the plan outright. 'It's beyond the poor to instruct others. They'll soon think themselves as good as everyone else.'

Some of the ladies laughed over their fans. 'Poor Miss Nagle! Have you heard her latest scheme? Whoever heard such nonsense! The poor instructing others!'

'I am also concerned about her educating the poor girls to read and write. Whatever will they do with these skills? All they need to learn is how to clean, mend and cook,' Mrs Blake announced with authority.

The women nodded in unison.

'Mr Jones was saying exactly the same last night,' Mrs Jones agreed.

'I think they should also learn laundry skills. I don't know what I would do without my laundrywomen,' Mrs Dickson added.

At the appalling thought of no servants, the women were plunged into silence for a whole minute.

A few of the wealthy men discussed the issue of Nano sending her boys to the West Indies. 'A fine woman, Miss Nagle. She has revolutionised the streets; but her imagination has carried her away this time.'

An undeterred Nano began her work of educating poor young men for her missionary work, which proved so successful she could write to Miss Fitzsimons in early 1770:

I am sending boys to the West Indies. Some charitable gentlemen have put themselves to great expense to help. All my children are brought up to be fond of instructing, as I think it is in the power of the poor to be of more service that way than the rich. My children tell me they will take great pains with the children over there to instruct them. Next year I will have pictures for them to give. I must beg you be so kind as to buy me some dozens of pictures for them.

December 1770 ended as a year of mixed blessings. One of Nano's greatest joys was to hear that Mary Kavanagh was enjoying teaching in the Ursuline Poor School. She was so successful there that Nano was worried that she might decide to remain in Paris. The fear, fortunately, was unfounded. The news that her cousin, Margaret Nagle, was suffering from nervous fits was of a deeper concern. Nano firmly believed that the tensions caused by the attitude of the Jansenistic novice mistress, Sister Saint Joseph, were at the root of Margaret's problems. She wrote to Eleanor that she lamented she had not been aware of the Jansenistic influence in the novitiate. She assured the worried Eleanor that once Margaret returned to Cork her health would improve, and she would be an excellent mistress for the poor children. Eleanor had also expressed concern over Elizabeth Coppinger, who was unsettled because she had not heard from her family. The daily dangers faced by prominent families like the Coppingers were never far from people's minds. Nano, understanding this, hastened to tell Eleanor that she had heard from the Coppingers the day before, and all was well with them. She sent her own affectionate thoughts and compliments to Eleanor.

After receiving Eleanor's letter, Nano believed that all was not running as smoothly as it should in the training of her novices. Father Doran, who shared her uneasiness, braved personal dangers to travel to Paris to discover what was really happening. He found that differences among the Ursuline superiors about the Cork foundation were causing problems; for this reason, he advised Nano to transfer her novices home as quickly as possible.

'Oh dear,' Nano sighed when she read Father Doran's letter. Poor Eleanor and my novices! I'll arrange to have them here as soon as I can – and I must write to Eleanor of my longing for their homecoming. In the letter to Eleanor, she acknowledged her own impatience for their arrival, adding, 'I must say, every disappointment we have had the Almighty has been pleased to make it turn out to our advantage, and when you come here, by degrees and with the assistance of God we may do a great deal.'

To comply with the requirements of canon law, it was essential that a professed Ursuline sister would accompany the Irish novices to Cork. Nano had no doubts that this would occur, especially when one Ursuline, in whom Nano expressed great confidence, had expressed her desire to do so. To Nano's disappointment however, because of their uncertainty about the success of the foundation, the superiors refused their permission. There was one bright note – the Ursuline Novice Mistress, who had been reluctant to profess the Irish novices, had a change of heart about this and was now allowing them to be professed.

The Ursuline Novice Mistress stated: 'The novices have a thorough knowledge of the rule, have practised the exercises of the institute and have truly imbibed its spirit. I am confident they will be worthy and courageous Ursuline Sisters. They have expressed a strong desire to be professed in Ireland. In my opinion this is a very rash wish.'

After consultation, however, the superiors decided that the novices be allowed to make their profession in Cork. Because of their grave misgivings about the whole enterprise, it was somewhat of a relief for them that the profession would take place in Cork, thus alleviating any of their feelings of responsibility when it all failed. They also consistently refused to allow a superior to go with them.

The novices, Eleanor (now Sister Angela), Mary Nagle (Sister Joseph), Elizabeth Coppinger (Sister Augustine) and Mary Kavanagh (Sister Ursula), were overjoyed that their request to be professed in Cork would be respected. The idea of a religious profession in Penal Ireland was almost beyond belief. Nano's pride and joy, too, knew no bounds. She wrote to Eleanor:

My dear Miss Fitzsimons,
I cannot express my pride and joy in you all. Your decision to be professed in Cork is beyond my hopes. I would never have had the temerity to suggest it. You will never know how much I long for your return.

Give my best regards to the Superior and to your mistress and my affectionate compliments to all the young ladies.
Your affectionate friend,
Nano Nagle

Having been unsuccessful in his search for a superior, Father Moylan, who was in Paris to accompany the novices home, turned in desperation to one of his clergy friends. They suggested that he approach Mother Margaret Kelly, who lived in the Ursuline convent in Dieppe.

The night before his appointment with Mother Margaret, Father Moylan pleaded with God that her heart would be moved by Nano's story and her struggles for the Irish people.

The next morning, after the usual pleasantries, he came to the point of his visit. 'Mother Margaret, I know you have already heard so much about Miss Nagle's bravery and how she has dedicated her whole life and her fortune to help the disadvantaged in Cork, and you know why I am here.'

'Indeed I do, Father,' she replied. 'As you are aware, I was born in Ireland and do have relatives there, which I am sure you also know. Like you, the Nagle children, and many others whose parents could afford it, I was educated in France. Unlike many others I have remained in France, joined the Ursulines and have been professed for twenty-five years. I see from your expression that you are aware of this too. I do admire Miss Nagle and her work, but I am sorry to say I would not be a suitable person as a superior in Cork. I have been away from Ireland nearly all my life, and from what I hear I would not be capable of handling the conditions there. To be truthful, I would be too fearful, and I am not sure that the foundation will be successful. I don't think I could deal with that. Please pass on my prayers for the success of her work to Miss Nagle.'

Father Moylan cajoled, argued and pleaded, but to no avail – Mother Margaret remained adamant in her refusal. Convinced that Mother Margaret was the right person to accompany the novices as superior, Father Moylan made an appointment to see the Bishop of Rouen, under whose jurisdiction the Ursulines in Dieppe were. The Archbishop listened sympathetically to this earnest young priest, whose work with the Parisian poor he was familiar.

'Father Moylan, although we understood why you needed to go, we were sad when you decided to return to your homeland. I will always hold in high esteem the young Irish men who have been educated in France for the purpose of returning as priests, and many who have suffered, some death, for that decision. You are one such man, who has suffered, but fortunately have escaped death.'

'Your Grace, I was very happy in France and loved my time in Paris. I am pleased to hear that you understood my need to return to Cork. You know my Uncle, Father Doran, who is there too, sends his regards, and asks that you kindly remember him and all the Jesuits in your prayers.'

'I am afraid we are on the road to persecution here, too. The expulsion of the Jesuits has been a great blow to us. Some are foretelling the closure of convents will be next. That brings me to your request that Mother Kelly accompany you to Cork. Can you give me some certainty that she will be safe there, and that Miss Nagle has the finance to support her foundation?'

'Indeed, Your Grace, I can assure you on both issues. Miss Nagle has had no problems with her schools and has taken every precaution that the foundation will be safe. She is renowned for her prudence. As for her finances, she is extremely wealthy, and seems to be gifted in all areas of finance. I know that even her brothers have had occasion to borrow from her. Have no fear, she is a most remarkable woman.'

Father Moylan left the Archbishop with high hopes.

Happy with what he had heard, the Archbishop arranged to meet Mother Kelly the following day. He told her, 'Mother Kelly, you have proven to be a most worthy daughter of the Ursuline Sisters and have given twenty-five years of wonderful service. They tell me you show good leadership qualities. I am sure you are not wanting in courage. I do not need to remind you about your vow of obedience when I ask you to accompany Father Moylan to Cork as superior of this fledgling community.'

Mother Margaret Kelly had no option but to prepare for her departure to Cork. In mid April 1771 Father Moylan wrote to Nano:

Dear Miss Nagle,

It gives me great pleasure to tell you that we are all ready to come to Cork. The novices are overjoyed, especially Sister Angela, whose patience and fortitude have been exemplary. Although Mother Margaret still expresses doubts over her ability to lead this little group, she is doing all she can to prepare herself, and to make sure all our endeavours are a success. We plan to leave Paris in the near future for the Carmelite convent of St Denis, where almost every member is Irish, all of whom have been enthusiastic supporters of this venture. From there we will travel to Rouen, where we will be joined by Mother Margaret, and where the sisters will change into secular dress, which you and I agree will be essential before we enter Ireland. I know you are very particular about this, and are praying that we will be able to enter Ireland without the discovery of these women being religious sisters. Our last stop will be Havre, where, weather permitting, we will board for Ireland.

We rely on your prayers for a safe journey.

I am your devoted servant,

Francis Moylan

For fear of the letter falling into dangerous hands, he gave it into the keeping of his half-brother, Jaspar Moylan, who was travelling back to Cork.

On receiving this welcome news a week or so later, Nano went to check on the new convent, going from room to room inspecting furniture, fixtures and even the garden.

'Thank God I spent those months in the Ursuline convent,' she told her foreman, 'I now know exactly what is expected. You have done well with these rooms, and I particularly like the chapel. Your workmen have carried out my instructions on the prie-dieux, John. I hope the Ursulines will be as happy as I am.'

Satisfied that all was ready, Nano anxiously awaited their arrival. 'I do hope all will go well when the sisters arrive,' she confided to Mary. 'At this stage it would be a tragedy if their identity and mission were discovered. We must pray for their safety Mary.'

'Indeed Miss Nagle, we are all praying for their safe arrival and their success. As you and I know, some of the teachers are growing too old for this type of work. We know, too, how difficult it is for you to find and train teachers, so we will all be happy if these sisters arrive. Is it true that they also teach the wealthy? This will be a great help to the merchants too, if they are brave enough to send the girls to be educated by them.'

'Yes, they do mainly teach the wealthy, but are also committed to the poor. As for people sending their girls to be educated by them, I really cannot answer that question, though I believe they will, because they have braved many other issues,' Nano answered. 'Mary, I have just leased another site, which will enable the sisters to have more room, and gardens in which they can spend their recreation time. Mrs Robbins and I signed the agreement yesterday.'

'I don't think I have met anyone as thoughtful as you, Miss Nagle,' Mary said.

CHAPTER NINE

Hearing the knock, Nano opened the front door. Father O'Halloran stood there, his face wreathed in smiles. He could not wait to enter the house to tell her the news.

'Wonderful news, Nano! Father Moylan and the sisters, although delayed by storms, have landed at Cove. I knew you were anxious, so I came immediately to tell you that they will be here sometime later today.'

'Do come in, Father, and thank you so much. The cousins, Sisters Augustine and Ursula, asked permission to stay for a few days at their relatives, the Coppingers at Rossmore, which is on their way to Cork from the harbour. The others, I believe, will come straight here. Oh! What a marvellous day.'

When Father O'Halloran had left, Nano made haste to the schools and the building site to share the good news. Once there, she went from room to room once more, and questioned the foreman about the day when the building would be habitable.

'The sisters can stay with me for a short time,' Nano told him, 'but, as you are aware, my house is rather small to accommodate so many people.'

'Don't worry, Miss Nagle, if the weather stays fine enough we should soon be ready for the sisters to settle in.'

With this assurance, Nano had to be satisfied. She hurried home where she waited anxiously for the sound of the carriage that would bring the sisters. Clop! Clop! It wasn't long before she heard it – the horses' hooves on the cobbles. Nano opened the door and warmly greeted Mother Margaret Kelly, then saw for the first time her first novice, Sister Angela Fitzsimons – tall, imposing, serene and with a most dazzling smile. Nano was enveloped in a warm hug. Behind her came her little cousin, now Sister Joseph, who beamed at Nano. Thank God she looks happy and in good health, Nano thought.

'I cannot express how happy I am that you have all arrived safely and well, and how welcome you all are. My dream has been achieved – and how appropriate it is that it is Ascension Day!' Nano told them.

After the sisters settled into their cramped quarters and shared a meal together, there was much chatter and sharing of news, until Nano declared that they should retire and continue their conversation in the days to come.

'Tomorrow I shall take you to see your new convent and introduce you to the foreman. If you are not too weary after your long journey we could also see my first school, which is in the confines of the convent, but perhaps we should leave the other schools for other days. Would that be convenient for you?'

'Thank you, Miss Nagle. We are anxious to see the convent and the school, but perhaps, as you suggest, we could leave the other schools until a later date, especially as I am sure the other novices would like to be with us when we go,' Mother Margaret answered for them all.

Within five weeks of their arrival, their first postulant, Eleanor Daly, entered. Nano, familiar with the family, had no qualms about approving this young lady from Cork. What an asset to teaching and religious life she will be, thought Nano, and such a sign of hope for the growth of this congregation.

The soft autumn sun on the morning of 18 September 1771 added to the joy in Nano's little house. Today was moving day. All were up early to give praise for a day longed for by so many for so long. The Ursuline Sisters, singing the *Te Deum*, took possession of their convent. Although Sister Angela was noted for her magnificent singing voice, none had heard it ring out so joyfully or so angelically as on this day. In Nano's heart there was a song of equal joy and thankfulness. After many hours of prayer and thought Nano had formulated a deed of agreement, which, after the Mass celebrated by Bishop Butler, she and Mother Margaret signed, witnessed by a proud Bishop Butler and a delighted Father Moylan. Later in the day, while sitting with her Ursuline Sisters, Nano reflected that it was the happiest day of her life.

'What an impressive day,' Mother Margaret agreed. She looked at the little group about her. Sitting beside her was Nano, her faced transformed by happiness; next were the four eager novices.

Nano smiled and nodded, waiting to hear the others' reflection. She was not disappointed.

'I was so pleased to see Bishop Butler looking so proud about us being here, and didn't he look magnificent?' Sister Augustine responded.

Sister Angela commented, 'I was happy that the Bishop recognised the interest and hard work of Father Moylan by appointing him our ecclesiastical director. I don't really know Father Shortall, whom he appointed our chaplain, but perhaps you do, Miss Nagle?'

'Yes, he is a Jesuit priest, who came here after their expulsion from France,' Nano answered. 'We are so fortunate to have the Jesuits who have been brave, dedicated and supportive of all our works with the poor.' Nano looked affectionately at these young enthusiastic women. How pleased she was to have them here at last.

'Miss Nagle, before the day ends I would like you to tell us which room you would prefer. We are so looking forward to you living with us now we are settled in this splendid convent you have provided for us,' Mother Margaret asked.

Nano looked a little surprised, then answered kindly but firmly.

'Mother Margaret, I am sorry if I have misled you, but I won't be moving here. This is your home now, where I hope that each of you will be very happy, and of course safe. I will remain in my cottage but will always support you.'

There was disappointment on every face.

'Miss Nagle,' began Mother Margaret, but before she could continue Nano raised her hand. 'No,' she smilingly said. 'Thank you to each one, but I have made my decision.'

With that the Ursulines said no more that night. For them, however, it was not finalised. Over the next week or so, after Nano left for work they moved her bed into their convent to a room they had prepared for her, and each evening, Nano quietly had it moved back again.

'It's only right that a foundress should live in her convent,' Sister Angela protested.

Eventually, dispirited, the Ursulines gave up.

'We all know Miss Nagle is a woman who knows her own mind,' Mother Margaret told the novices. 'We really must respect her wishes.'

Disappointed, the novices made no further attempts to move Nano into the convent.

Mother Margaret, concerned about Nano's frailty, spoke to her. 'Miss Nagle, we respect your decision, but ask that you allow us to prepare a daily meal for you. That is one way in which we can show our appreciation for all you do for us.'

Nano quickly perceived the Ursulines' need to express their affection and gratitude, and replied, 'Thank you, Mother. I must admit I am not the greatest cook, so I would appreciate a meal.'

When she heard this Sister Angela sighed with relief. 'At least we now know Miss Nagle will be assured of one good meal a day. I have always been so worried about her health. You know two of her sisters died young and she has a weak chest. I often wonder when she gets time to cook for herself. We can all see how frail she is.'

'I don't think she considers herself at all,' Sister Joseph added.

Both Sisters Ursula and Elizabeth looked worried. 'She does look very fragile, and I've heard her coughing on foggy days,' the former observed.

'Yes,' added Sister Elizabeth. 'Have you seen her arrive home on a wet day? Her cloak and bonnet drip, her shoes are sodden and she looks absolutely frozen. It's amazing that none of us have ever heard her complain.'

'As she is my cousin, I know she is extremely wealthy. It is almost beyond understanding how she spends so little money, or even any time, on herself,' Sister Joseph remarked.

'I am awed at the thought of her bravery,' Sister Ursula observed. 'I couldn't walk around the lanes like she does, especially after dark.'

'I couldn't even do it in broad daylight,' interjected Sister Joseph. 'I'd be too frightened to even run if I saw men brandishing knives and fighting. I think I would scream my head off, and I don't know what I would do if I saw the press gang rushing towards me.'

The others laughed at her horrified expression.

'I'm going to make sure she receives a good, nourishing meal at least once a day, and I'm going to keep an eye on her health,' Sister Angela announced.

The evenings were becoming shorter and the weather more uncertain, but on this evening, although the shadows were long, the breath of the breeze which whispered about the house was still kind. Nano sat at her desk to write the long overdue letter to her family in Bath.

My dear David and Mary, Joseph and Frances,

Words cannot express my happiness. My heart is no longer troubled about the future of my beloved schools and the poor, for the Ursulines have moved into their convent where, I am pleased to say, they are quite comfortable and very safe. They have already received one postulant, with more women making enquiries.

As I know Uncle Joseph would have advised, I have devised a written agreement to ensure my schools and works would continue as I have always planned. I realise that in Penal Law we Catholics cannot make legal contracts, but to us who are involved, this agreement is legally binding. I know, David and Joseph, you will like to know the terms which I set out, so will describe them briefly, and I am sure you will approve.

To help the sisters settle in, I endowed them with an initial sum of £2,000. Because I believe it to be essential that I direct them, as they are all young and inexperienced in the culture and life of Cork City, I informed them that I wished to be acknowledged as their foundress and have the right of nominating subjects for my lifetime. I may, in time, wish to join them, but if that is so, I have insisted that I be received without any of my wealth except a yearly pension.

The Ursulines, on their part, undertook to offer Mass annually on the 24 April for Uncle Joseph, and to observe my requests for the celebration of my funeral, which I will not bore you with at this time. While we were discussing the content of the agreement, I was pleased that they wished to acknowledge Father Moylan's persistence and dedication in making the foundation, by committing to offer general Holy Communion for him in perpetuity on the Feast of Saint Francis.

Bishop Butler, who has been so supportive, has officially appointed Father Moylan Ecclesiastical Director and Mother Margaret Kelly as superior. I know you will all share my happiness. It is a day which will be forever etched in my memory.

I hope each of you is in good health and still enjoying the life of peace in Bath.

Your affectionate sister,

Nano

Nano's step was lighter and her heart filled with joy as she walked along the lanes, visiting the schools where the children were being prepared for their new teachers. The teachers who had been with Nano for some years were pleased that they would be supported by the sisters, while the younger ones would be happy to have them as guides. The teachers' spokesperson, Mary Fouhy, told Nano, 'Miss Nagle, like you, we have been apprehensive that, after all the years we have spent in sustaining your school system, it would not last. We have all seen the closure of so many schools once their patron died. Such a fate has been a painful thought for us, and we know it has been troublesome for you. We are now so delighted and relieved for you that your work will continue, and are comforted that the young teachers have security of employment in a work to which they are so committed.'

A gratified Nano answered, 'I know Mary. I don't think I have thanked you all sufficiently, but I have always been aware of the daily dangers you all face so courageously and how you work with love. I can never thank each of you enough.'

'You have been a wonderful role model to us and the children, indeed to everyone, Miss Nagle. We have had only one concern and that was for your health. The teachers asked me to tell you of their affection and admiration, Miss Nagle.'

Mary was usually a woman of few words, so Nano was quite overcome. There flashed through her mind the fears, frustrations, failures, the joys and successes, small and great, and the hopes they had all shared.

'Mary,' she murmured, 'we have had to struggle. Now we can dream of a better future for my works.'

The Ursulines began teaching in Nano's Poor School, which fell within the confines of their convent walls. They made no attempt, however, to go to teach in any of the other schools.

'Do you know when the sisters are going to come to teach in any of the other schools, Miss Nagle?' Mary asked one day.

'I was wondering that myself, Mary. However, I feel we must be patient as the sisters have not been here long, and although they have women requesting to join them, they will need time to become accustomed to this new situation. Bishop Butler has already written to Rome requesting that the canonical time in the novitiate be shortened to allow the profession of the novices, so perhaps we will know then. You have no doubt heard that Father Moylan's half-sister Mary has returned from Paris to join the Ursulines.'

'No, I had not heard that, but it is all good news.'

'Miss Nagle, we are opening our school which at present can only accommodate twelve girls, and we would love you to be present for our opening,' Mother Margaret told Nano one morning.

Nano congratulated her Ursuline Sisters and accepted their invitation, adding, 'I see that the girls in the Poor School are progressing with their reading, writing, arithmetic and needlework, too. You are doing great work with them. I do hope we hear from Rome soon so that you can extend your work.'

The twelve girls from wealthy mercantile families settled in happily. Nano came each evening to the room set aside for her, to help instruct them in their faith. How different this all is from my first encounter with the street children, Nano thought.

'Miss Nagle, how are you finding our students?' Sister Angela asked after an evening session.

With a wide smile Nano answered, 'Sister Angela, you will never know how terrified I was in those early days. The smells! The language!' Nano shuddered as she remembered. 'Now I love my work; in fact, I take such pleasure in it that I may never get to heaven! The girls here are all so anxious to learn that I am sure their parents will be happy with their progress. I know I am.'

It wasn't long after this conversation that the city fathers, or the D'Oyer Hundred, expressed alarm about the Ursuline foundation, believing it to be a threat to the Protestant security of the city. When Nano opened the *Freeman's Journal* on 18 February 1772 she was alarmed to read an anonymous letter warning of a brewing papist plot: 'Three new Catholic chapels have been built and there are swarms of Jesuits and nuns from France in the city for the purpose of making converts of young and weak minds. There's a Popish nunnery with French connections in Cove Lane.'

Nano was aware that her worst fears seemed about to be realised. She hastened to the convent with the paper. 'We must be careful, sisters,' she cautioned them. 'I have heard that the Council of the D'Oyer Hundred has convened a meeting in the Guildhall tonight to consider closing the convent and the school.'

'Thank you for warning us, Mother Nagle,' Mother Margaret said. 'Like you, we believe prayer can move mountains, so that is what we will do.'

'Yes,' Nano agreed, but added sardonically, 'I hope you pray earnestly, but hope you do more than that. It is also best that you don't wear your habits, even in the house.' It was an anxious night for Nano and the sisters.

It was a great relief the next day when Father Moylan arrived to tell them the news.

'I hear there were a few members who were quite vocal about the suppression of the convent and school. One member went so far as to accuse you of trying to convert Protestants.'

'Surely not!' Mother Margaret objected.

'I'm afraid so. However, Francis Carlton – you've no doubt heard of him, he's sometimes called 'King Carlton'?' the sisters nodded. 'Well, he called for a little common sense.'

At this there was a general sigh of relief.

'What did he say, Father?' Nano queried.

'He pointed out that if they suppressed the convent, the mercantile families would once again send their children overseas for education, and if that happened, money now spent in the city would be spent overseas. Cork City can ill afford to suffer any more economic losses, he reminded them.'

'They wouldn't want to lose any money,' Nano commented dryly.

'I think he must have a sense of humour, which you would appreciate, Nano, because he concluded his argument by remarking that he was sure no harm could come from some pious ladies who met together, said their rosaries and drank tea!'

They all laughed.

He had gone when Nano thoughtfully told the sisters, 'Although this incident has passed, we can never be sure when and where intolerance will raise its head, so it is wise to be always cautious. I ask again that you never wear your habits. I know it is a wish of yours to do so, but I must stress that you never be seen in them.'

Not long after this incident Nano and Mother Margaret were informed that Bishop Butler had received news from Rome, and that Father Moylan wished to meet with them.

As he approached, Nano, who knew him so well, observed with apprehension his solemn expression.

After their preliminary greetings, Father Moylan said, 'Nano, on Bishop Butler's request on your behalf, the Holy Father has released you from the vow you made to enter religious life and gives his consent that you make a vow of perpetual chastity. We hope you will be happy with this. The other piece of good news is that Rome has agreed to reduce to one year the term before religious profession in your convent, until your number reaches twelve members, when it will revert to two years.'

'Wonderful news, Father!' both women exclaimed. 'We will certainly thank the Bishop for his efforts to obtain it.'

Before they could continue, Father Moylan dampened their spirits.

'Unfortunately,' he interrupted, 'the laws of enclosure will remain the same as in Paris. You will not be going out to the Poor Schools as we had planned. I am sorry we can do no more about this.'

'But surely the Holy Father knows what happens here in Ireland! If the law could be relaxed for some other places, why can it not here?' Mother Kelly said in a shocked voice.

Father Moylan looked with compassion at Nano, who was so appalled she was bereft of speech. Disappointment flashed across her face, followed by anger. He could see her struggle to maintain a calm demeanour and was too afraid to say anything further. He could actually think of nothing to say, even though on the way he had rehearsed so many speeches he could make to her. Eventually Nano spoke. 'Thank you, Father, for all your efforts, although I cannot understand Rome's decision in this matter.' She turned to Mother Margaret. 'This does not alter my decision to support you all in any way I can, Mother Margaret.'

'Mother Nagle, you will continue to come to teach the girls, won't you? You know we have set aside that small room for your use so please do come, won't you?'

Although Nano felt that her heart was broken, she nodded and smiled.

With his heart divided between happiness for the Ursulines' future and disappointment for Nano, Father Moylan relayed to the Bishop the outcome of the visit. After his and Nano's departure, Mother Margaret shared the news with the sisters, whose joy that their profession could take place soon was overshadowed by their disappointment about the enclosure. All, especially Sister Angela, felt Nano's grief. How she could bear this continued thwarting of her dreams was uppermost in their minds.

Nano walked slowly home through the depressing drizzle and darkness. Her thoughts and feelings mirrored the weather. It had never seemed depressing before. She looked at the meal so lovingly prepared for her by Sister Angela. How could she eat it? She felt so old and tired. What was she to do? She looked again at the food, noticing that Sister Angela had cooked her favourite things. She thought of Sister Angela's fortitude and bravery over the years, of her spending time that day thinking of how she could tempt her to eat this evening meal after such woeful news. Dear Angela, she thought, how can I be so ungrateful? She took up the meal, which at first had no taste for her, and gradually, as she felt warmer, her thoughts became more positive. I must write the news to my brothers, and to Miss Mulally, to whom I owe a letter. But not tonight.

She couldn't help being a little cross in her talk to God that night, but by the end she came to the conclusion that God had always provided, and always would.

Nano sat bolt upright in bed. There was no light to seep into her bedroom. There was no noise on the street. I must have been dreaming, she concluded. She had seen her father conversing with Uncle Joseph, who said, 'Garrett, don't worry. We both know that Nano always finds a way to do what God wants.'

There, too she had seen golden-haired Catherine and Ann with her sweet smile, both of whom nodded. 'Yes, Papa, don't you remember?' asked Ann.

Nano relived the dream. She felt a determination to continue, so, as it was nearly time to rise, she did so, and set off through the fog to Saint Finbarr's for her hour's prayer before Mass. Yes, if it's God's work there must be a way, she thought. Afterwards, she felt a deep peace and a certainty that somehow she would find a solution for the continuation of her works.

Before she could write her letters she received one from Teresa Mulally.

Dear Miss Nagle,

When Father Moylan was here last he informed me of the arrival of your Ursulines. I rejoice with you. I know you are always interested in my work here, which I have modelled on your own. The girls are progressing well in their knowledge and skills. As you advised, we teach them their prayers and the catechism. We instruct them in writing, reading, knitting, quilting, mantua making and plain work. Our programme is very similar to the one you have for your schools. Our appeal for funds, about which I wrote you, was very successful and we appointed Mrs Coppinger as our patron.

As you know, spies and informers are always on the prowl, so I have to walk warily. In the front room we teach the girls knitting, sewing and the like, and in the back room catechism, reading, writing and arithmetic. If danger looms the children stow away the evidence of learning and move to the front room, where they are seen busily learning how to turn a heel or close a toe.

I don't think I told you that I have now two helpers, a Miss Ann Corballis and a Miss Judith Clinch. Something else I learnt from you, Miss Nagle, is to send the children home in small groups and at intervals, to prevent their attracting notice.

I have one hundred poor girls in my school where, like you, I provide food and clothing. At the present time I am thinking of opening a small boarding school for poor abandoned orphan girls. I will be only able to accept five, but at least that is a beginning.

I assure you of my sincere love and gratitude,
Teresa Mulally

Nano sat down and took up her pen to reply to Teresa. There was so much to tell and it would be a relief to share her disappointment with her old friend.

Dear Miss Mulally,
I read with happiness your letter, which I received recently. It gives me great pleasure to hear of the work you do for the children of your school. I wish you every success for your boarding school. Father Moylan told me you had been ill, but, as you did not mention it, I hope that you have recovered.

Mother Margaret and the Ursuline Sisters have settled into their convent well, and are already establishing a good name for themselves as skilled teachers and dedicated religious. Several talented and devout young ladies have expressed a desire to join them as Ursuline Sisters, all of which promise well for their future. The first to apply was an Eleanor Daly, whom you would not know as she comes from Cork. The second is Mary Moylan, who you remember was interested in entering in France but did not. She has now rethought her decision and, to her half-brother Father Moylan's delight, she has entered here. As both young women are intelligent, bright and devout, I have approved their application. I am disappointed and saddened that they are unable to leave their enclosure to work with the poor of the city, especially the poor children in my schools. I am consoled with the thought that they are the first religious congregation in Ireland to devote themselves to the instruction of girls, and particularly the education of the wealthy. You cannot imagine the relief and joy of the parents who do not have to face the dangerous prospect of sending their daughters to the Continent for education. The girls, too, appreciate that they are not separated from their families and have to live in a strange land for so many years. Now that we have the first religious congregation to work in our country since the Penal Laws were imposed, I have great hopes for the future – if we are brave enough to take the steps needed.

I am hoping that you will take time to visit us in Cork, where I would be delighted to have you stay in my small home.

Your affectionate friend,
Nano Nagle

As she had done before the arrival of the Ursulines, Nano continued to walk the lanes and alleyways, to climb the rickety, sometimes board-rotted stairs to the attics housing the poor, to visit the prisons and workhouses, and to visit her schools on a daily basis. Over the decades little seemed to have changed for a great number of the poor. As the children from her schools bettered themselves and their families, their places were taken by victims of famine and displacement from the country. If only she could increase the number of her schools, instead of worrying about how they would continue.

One evening Mary Fouhy remarked on how tired she looked. 'Mary, I delight so much in my schools, and in excellent teachers like you and little Miss Elizabeth Burke, but I am saddened when I have to dismiss someone who thinks more of money than the children's education. As you know, I am becoming more concerned about the future of all my works, but especially my schools, now that the Ursulines are unable to help us.'

'We have seen so many Charter and Charity Schools close when their patrons died or their funds dried up, that we share your concerns. Elizabeth and I were discussing this yesterday, Miss Nagle, and we are confident that God will guide you with an inspiration.'

'Mary, you are reminding me that I have often said that God will provide, so I must continue to have hope and belief,' Nano said with a wry smile.

'Yes, indeed, Miss Nagle. It is a bitter disappointment for you that the Ursulines have to devote most of their efforts to teaching the wealthy. None of us can imagine the amount of money you have spent on their education, convent building, travel from France and the money with which you still support them. I'm not even mentioning the time and effort you spent in planning and dreaming. Who could blame you for feeling disappointed?'

'As I have told Sister Angela, the Almighty permits everything for the best. I know the Ursulines are doing – and will continue to do – great work. I must again think of a way to ensure the continuation of my schools and my work with the poor.'

This desire became the focus of Nano's thoughts and her talks with God. The candlelight played mischievously on the cottage walls. The city, unusually mist-free, had quietened, and all was enveloped in darkness as Nano finished the meal provided for her by the devoted Sister Angela. Nano knelt to have her usual prayers before retiring to bed. Her sore knees had barely touched the prie-dieu when she was startled by a thought. Why not found her own religious congregation? Why not, she wondered. All thoughts of her sore knees and aching bones were replaced by feelings of energy and light-heartedness.

On this and following nights she spent her God talk time on these thoughts. Sadly, Father Doran, who had died in 1771, was no longer there with his fatherly advice, but Father Moylan and Bishop Butler, especially the former, would be consulted. She would stress that it was important that her work on the streets, and in the attics, prisons, hospitals and workhouses as well as in the Poor Schools, would continue, and if possible expand. She had not forgotten her plans to build a home for elderly destitute women, one for elderly men, and of course a home for prostitutes. This must all be pointed out. I'll personally need to choose some young women to join me, too. In her mind she began to meticulously plan, and when she felt sufficiently prepared, she arranged to meet with Father Moylan, now parish priest.

'Do come in, Father,' she greeted him when he arrived, punctually as usual.

'Thank you. I notice that your step is lighter these last couple of weeks, so I presume you have good news for me. Is it word from Bath?' he asked.

'I have a new project I wish to discuss with you, Father,' Nano smilingly replied.

At this Father Moylan looked a little apprehensive. I wonder what this is, he thought. I hope it won't be too challenging, but nothing would surprise me.

It was challenging and it did surprise him.

Nano, who could read his thoughts, smiled to herself.

'You know how worried I have been about the future of my works, especially my schools, Father,' she began.

'Oh! Come Nano!' He tended to be very protective of the Ursulines, where he now had several relatives. 'We are all disappointed about their enclosure, but no one can complain about their wonderful work with young women and girls from the mercantile families, who you know are overjoyed with them. I've been to their Poor School, where they are also doing great work. The sisters are so admired and appreciated that many girls are asking to join them, so they are already planning building additions.'

Nano stopped the flow of words by agreeing, 'Yes, Father, they are doing wonderful work. Of course I am pleased that their numbers are growing, and they also care for me each day; but I did not ask you here to discuss the Ursuline Sisters.'

Father Moylan again looked worried. Nano continued. 'I have decided to establish a religious society which will devote itself entirely to the poor. It will carry on my work in the schools and with the poor wherever they are found.'

Father Moylan was startled into silence. He had imagined Nano calling him for many reasons, but not this. Nano waited patiently through the silence for his reply, but she knew that, whatever it was, her resolve would not weaken.

Eventually he said in a weak voice, 'Nano, you have surprised me. Have you thought through what you are proposing? As for me, there are so many obstacles to this plan that I don't know where to start.'

'I have thought deeply about this, Father, and have already begun to plan for its success.'

'I don't know, Nano. It is forbidden by law. It's too dangerous.' He saw Nano's implacable look. How well he knew it! He added with resignation: 'You will need to speak to the

Bishop about it as soon as possible.'

'Thank you, Father. I have already made an appointment to see him,' Nano replied.

Father Moylan took up his hat and thoughtfully walked home.

CHAPTER 10

Nano walked purposefully up the winding staircase. Everything gleamed. The marble steps, the mahogany hand rails – all spoke of opulence. Well, he is a prince of the Church and noble by birth, so I must not be critical, Nano reflected. And he has been a great supporter of the Ursuline foundation. At the top of the stairs the Butler coat of arms hanging on the wall told the story. Nano, who was quite familiar with it, glanced at it but was not intimidated. After all, her great-great-grandmother, Elizabeth Poyntz, had married Thomas Butler, and their eldest son became Duke of Ormond. On hearing her knock, the Bishop, who was expecting her, called in his melodious voice for her to enter.

From his ornately carved chair behind his equally ornately carved desk, the Bishop eyed the elderly, dark-clad lady who approached. He noticed that the grey tendrils of hair which had escaped from her simple cap were glistening from the outside damp, but what struck him most were the dark, lively eyes that seemed to pierce his thoughts, which he attempted to hide behind his affable welcome.

'Do be seated, Miss Nagle.' He pointed with a bejewelled finger to a plush velvet chair.

Nano murmured her thanks while she sat in the chair indicated, which was so big it almost enveloped her.

The Bishop steepled his hands. 'Now, Miss Nagle, I believe you wished to see me on a matter of great import. As I have an important function to attend, and my time is limited, perhaps you would like to tell me what it is.'

'Yes, My Lord, I do have something to discuss with you. It is about a religious congregation.'

'Oh yes,' the Bishop interrupted. 'I believe the Ursulines are doing great work in the city. You know that I have relatives who have entered there, and they seem very happy. You are to be congratulated on having brought them here, and for continuing to support them. I hope you don't have any complaints against them.'

'No, no! Of course I don't, My Lord. I am very proud of their bravery and their success. My concerns are with the continuation of my Poor Schools and all my work with the dispossessed.'

Before she could elaborate, the Bishop interrupted again. 'Miss Nagle, we cannot complain about Rome. Their laws of enclosure are there to protect religious women from the evils of the world. Mother Church values her nuns too much to subject them to worldly influences.'

'Yes, My Lord,' Nano answered, tongue in cheek. She continued, 'I do appreciate all that you did to support the Ursuline foundation and my own taking of vows, especially your correspondence with Rome. What I have come to tell you is that I wish to found my own religious congregation, which will be directed totally to the needs of the poor.'

The Bishop looked at her. I must have misheard her, he thought.

'Miss Nagle, would you like to explain to me what you are proposing?'

'As you say, My Lord, the Ursulines are bound by enclosure, which prevents them from working with the poor where they are. I envisage founding a religious group of women who will not be enclosed behind a boundary wall, and whose only parameters are being close to the needs of the poor.'

The Bishop's steepled hands collapsed. He gazed in shock at the calm little woman facing him.

'Found a religious congregation! Here! In Ireland!' he stuttered. Nano nodded.

'Without enclosure!' he exclaimed. Nano nodded.

'You can't take religious vows without enclosure. Rome won't allow it. It's been the law since the Council of Trent. There are a few religious institutes without enclosure on the Continent, but they don't have official approval, so they won't last, of course. If you do take solemn vows without enclosure, you are not considered a real religious and therefore you have no stability or security. I'm sure you don't want that,' he concluded triumphantly.

'In that case, I'll have to think of another way to live as a religious congregation.'

'Miss Nagle, it can't be done. Those laws won't change.'

'Bishop, they are so out of date for our times. Surely Rome realises that?'

The Bishop looked at Nano's calm, determined face. It just can't be done, but I am unable to change her mind. I might as well give permission, but I will not encourage her; then, when it all fails she can only blame herself. She won't get a religious to lead the group anyway, or anyone to join her, he thought with satisfaction.

'Miss Nagle, I see you are committed to this so I won't stand in your way. I would stress however that anything you do must not detract from the Ursuline foundation, or endanger our lives.'

'Thank you, My Lord,' Nano said.

'Now, I am a busy man, so I'll ask the servant to see you out, but do keep me informed. I wish you well.'

When she had gone, he sank back in his chair. 'God help us,' he said to the empty room, 'another Joseph Nagle.' He daintily took a pinch of snuff to fortify himself against the thought, and rang for the valet to prepare him for the dinner with his nephew, Lord Dunboyne, who was in town. About an hour later he was on his way, powdered wig tied back at the right angle, his fine silk suit and waistcoat embroidered with chenille, white breeches bound below the knee over white stockings, and his round-toed shoes shining brilliantly. He knew he was dressed in the height of fashion. He tried to banish Miss Nagle from his mind, but somehow her proposal kept worming its way into his thoughts. She can't succeed, he tried to convince himself. But what if she did? No, she would never find a suitable person – no one would be brave enough to be part of such a scheme. He breathed a sigh of relief when he reached his destination, and all thoughts of Miss Nagle were dispelled by an entertaining evening.

While Nano happily watched the development of her Ursuline community, she continued to ponder how she could begin a congregation which would meet the needs of the poor. Who could lead it? Who would join it? How would it sustain itself financially when she was gone? What form would it take? Where and how would they live? There were no guidelines for her to follow. As the needs on the Continent differed from those in Ireland she could not find an answer there. She lived in a time of change when new worlds were opening up and old ways were no longer applicable. It was all very confusing. There seemed to be no answers. There were two constants though: her love for the poor and her complete dedication to and faith in God. These were her guiding lines. She attended and rejoiced at the reception into the Ursuline community of Miss Daley and Miss Moylan on 12 April, and of Miss Mary Teresa Stack on 19 July 1772. Both ceremonies were celebrated by a proud Bishop Butler and Father Moylan. In 1773 Mary Kavanagh's sister, Lucy, joined the Ursulines, whose future was now very secure.

Nano's friend Josephine had retired from teaching, but Nano was able to discuss matters with Mary Fouhy and Elizabeth Burke, both of whom had been thrilled to attend the Ursuline ceremonies.

'Oh! I thought it all so inspirational, and I could listen forever to Sister Angela's beautiful singing of the psalms,' Mary told her.

'Sister Angela does have a magnificent voice, and the Bishop looked absolutely splendid and seemed so proud of the sisters,' Elizabeth said.

'Yes, both Bishop Butler and Father Moylan are pleased with the growth of the Ursuline foundation, as I am, of course,' Nano responded.

She sighed. If only she had sisters to work in her schools, and with the poor, whose need never diminished.

Finally, Nano came to a decision. She would found the congregation and would lead it herself. She knew what she wanted, and more specifically, what she did not want. She would begin by choosing some companions and planning a convent building. By now she had confidence that she could do both – the Ursuline convent next door was proof enough. The first two people who came to her mind for her community were Mary Fouhy and little Elizabeth Burke, both of whom had worked with her for many years. They were familiar with her ideals and principles and had been a great support, as well as being devoted to the work, to the poor and to bringing about God's justice in the world where they lived.

On a spring morning in 1773 Mary and Elizabeth came, at Nano's request, to her unprepossessing house.

'I wonder what Miss Nagle wants of us? I've spent all night thinking. Perhaps she wants to open a new school?' Mary said to Elizabeth as they neared Nano's cottage.

'I really don't know, Mary,' Elizabeth replied. 'I hope it hasn't been a tragedy in one of the schools; so many children die, or are killed. I'll never get used to it,' Elizabeth replied in a worried voice.

Nano, with her usual hospitality, served them hot cakes and tea, because although it was early spring there was still a bite in the air.

'Miss Nagle, I didn't know you were such a proficient cook,' Mary said appreciatively.

Nano laughed. 'Mary, I wish I could claim I was, but I suppose I should be honest. Sister Angela Fitzsimons looks after me very well, so I can never eat all she provides for me. I am pleased to share with you and am happy that you have enjoyed your cakes. I'll be sure to tell her how much you appreciated her kind thoughts. Now, you both must be wondering why I have sent for you. I have shared with you for some years my disquiet over the future of the schools and the works I have for the poor, so it is only right that I now share my dream about the solution to my problems. I have experienced how dedicated and devout you both are and, of course, you have always been discreet and brave.'

Mary looked as though she was about to protest but Nano rapidly went on. 'You have heard me reflecting on founding a religious congregation which would be devoted entirely to the needs of the poor and would serve them where they are, but whose members would also be women of prayer and centred on a spiritual life. You know, too, that I have failed to find anyone who was able or willing to lead this congregation. In fact, you are perhaps sick of hearing me complain about it,' Nano chuckled.

Both Mary and Elizabeth smiled sympathetically. They did not speak as they were unsure where this conversation was going.

'Now I have made up my mind about what to do,' Nano continued.

Both women waited expectedly for Nano to continue.

'Unworthy as I may be, I have decided to lead the congregation myself,' Nano paused. 'I would love both of you to join me as my first two sisters. You may wish for time to think over this invitation, as I know it is a very big decision, but you have my complete trust and faith.'

Mary blinked with pleasure, while Elizabeth turned pale with trepidation. Dare I? she wondered. Nano looked searchingly at them both. They could see hope written on her face.

'Oh! Miss Nagle, I am so honoured. I really can't express how I feel; I don't think I merit this invitation,' Mary explained.

'Yes, indeed, it is an honour,' Elizabeth, having heard Mary's response, recovered some of her courage to reply. 'I hope I prove worthy of your trust, Miss Nagle. God will surely assist us if it is his work, as you are always telling us, Miss Nagle.'

Nano breathed a sigh of relief. 'My heartfelt thanks to both of you. You have both proved your love of God and have spent your lives working to improve the lives of the disadvantaged. According to canon law we need at least four women to begin a religious congregation, so I am planning to invite Miss Mary Anne Collins to join us. I know you have met her, as she often visits the schools, and is a great help to us. More importantly she is a well-educated young woman who is very devout, prayerful and devoted to the poor.'

'Isn't she the sister of the Franciscan priest, Father Michael Collins?' asked Elizabeth.

'Yes, and he's a fine young priest, too,' Nano answered.

'I am quite impressed with Miss Collins, Miss Nagle,' Mary remarked.

Elizabeth nodded in agreement.

'Perhaps you are wondering if we have the support of the Bishop,' Nano began. 'Yes, I did have an appointment with him. Although I think he believes my project will fail, he did not discourage me, and gave his somewhat reluctant permission. I know that he will support us if we continue our good work.'

'We will certainly do our best, Miss Nagle,' the two assured Nano. Over more cups of tea, the three women spent time discussing Nano's plans for the future, and each person's place in it.

The next day Nano arranged to meet Mary Anne Collins to lay before her the plans for the new congregation and the invitation to join. Like Mary and Elizabeth, Mary Anne was at first overcome with pleasure but was apprehensive. Nano assured her that she would support them all with their further education. 'We must be the best educators possible,' Nano told her.

'Perhaps you need time to discuss this with your family,' Nano suggested.

Mary Anne was torn between a desire to say yes immediately, and the more prudent approach to discuss it with her family, and particularly with her Franciscan brother. She decided on the latter, telling Nano that she would give her answer as soon as possible.

Nano was not particularly concerned about this, as she knew in her heart what the answer would be. Mary Anne need not have hesitated. Father Michael Collins had heard of Nano's work through his fellow Franciscan priests, in particular Father Callanan, Guardian of the Franciscan Friary in Little Cross Street. Father Michael and his parents were delighted with Mary Anne's wish.

'Miss Nagle, I have thought and prayed about your invitation, which I discussed with my family. I would find it a privilege to join you and the other two women. I hope you will forgive me, but I have commitments for the year. Would it be possible for me to join you all when I have fulfilled these commitments?' Mary Anne asked anxiously.

Nano was overjoyed. With a light heart she could now begin to implement her plans. In the midst of the bitter winter of January 1775, Mary Fouhy and Elizabeth Burke joined her in her cottage. It was extremely cramped, but they were prepared for that, as they were for the frugal lifestyle they observed. They were used to the daily regime of early morning Mass and prayer, then school at eight o'clock, Mass for the children where they could teach them the prayers and ritual, followed by dinner, which Nano provided for the children at twelve, then classes until five o'clock. That was not the end of schooling, as Nano had introduced classes later in the day for older girls and boys. Added to all this were visits to the abandoned, aged and ill in the hovels and on the streets. Never a day passed without their personal God talk time, from which they obtained their energy and inspiration.

When the winter cold reluctantly withdrew in 1775, the workmen laid the foundations for Nano's convent. Nano had already told the Ursulines about her plans for a new congregation. Mother Margaret, at that time still Reverend Mother, had warmly received the news, which she shared with the other sisters, but as she was planning her return to France her thoughts were occupied with her own decisions, which had priority over all else. In January, Bishop Butler had held the first canonical visitation, appointing Sister Augustine Coppinger as assistant superior and mistress of novices, Sister Ursula Kavanagh as zelatrice, Sister Joseph Nagle as depositary and Sister Angela Fitzsimons as mistress-general. All the sisters, basking in the joys of their successes and their assured future, accepted Nano's news happily, as they genuinely wished Mother Nagle every success. While the foundations of Nano's convent were being laid, Mother Kelly departed for France, leaving Sister Augustine in charge of the Ursuline foundation. Amidst all this interior activity and their enclosure, the Ursulines were not aware at first of the foundations being laid a mere hundred metres from them. They became quite alarmed at its proximity. Just when they were beginning to feel so secure, they now felt threatened. This convent would draw children from their own establishment. How would their Poor School survive? Nano's friend, Sister Angela, tried to assure them, without success, that Nano would never jeopardise their work. The newly appointed leaders spoke to Nano of their fears, which she explained were without foundation. The people she would serve were not those whom the Ursulines provided for so well. Surely by now they knew that she would always protect their safety and future? However, they were not appeased. They sent for Father Moylan, who listened to their fears, which he shared. He decided to act quickly before the walls rose too high.

The next morning, when Nano was at the building site speaking with her old friend the foreman, she saw Father Moylan purposely striding through the building materials, looking neither left nor right.

'Well, well!' she said to the foreman who, seeing Father Moylan's approach, quickly made his way to a group of workmen nearby. On the way he was trying to think of something to speak to them about, so that they would be diverted from what he thought would be a confrontation.

'Miss Nagle!' Father Moylan almost shouted, before realising that many ears and eyes were covertly watching and listening.

'Good morning, Father,' Nano quietly responded. She was pleased that Sister Angela had warned her of the Ursulines' continued disquiet, so that Father Moylan's visit was not entirely surprising.

Father Moylan looked about him. He was surprised at the advanced stage of the building, but then, Nano had always had a way with her workmen, and her popularity knew few boundaries. At this thought he became more furious. How dare she build so close to the Ursuline convent! He thought of the consternation of his half-sister and his cousins who dwelt there, and who worked so hard. All their work and dedication could be in danger.

He struggled to control his anger, but failed to entirely subdue it. He quickly came to the point of his visit.

'Miss Nagle, this is my parish! You have no right to build so close to the Ursuline Sisters. I forbid it. If you don't tell the workmen to stop immediately, I'll have others pull down your walls by the end of the day.'

Nano looked at him searchingly. She was deeply hurt by the attitudes of the Ursuline Sisters, and now Father Moylan. After all the years she had worked with them in trust and love, and had spent a fortune on their very existence, she found it difficult to believe all this opposition was happening. Father Moylan thought that Nano would respect his wishes, or in this case his orders, because in the past she had been respectful of his views and often been guided by them.

'Father, I'm sorry you feel that way. Yes, you are parish priest but that does not give you the right to tell a parishioner where he or she may build a home, which is what I am doing. I have always respected your wishes, however; if you really insist I will tell the workmen to stop, and I'll build my convent home elsewhere in Ireland, perhaps Dublin. Both places have been pleading with me to make a foundation there, and we must admit the needs in both places are really great.'

A muffled snigger from a group of apprentices captured the foreman's attention. He stared at the group, who were all innocently concentrated on mixing the straw and clay for the bricks. I'll bet, he thought, the ringleader was that young red-headed Ryan, whose family came from Tipperary to escape the Famine. He, together with a couple of the other young apprentices, would be on their way to the gallows or the hulks now if it weren't for Miss Nagle. Rogues though they can be, Miss Nagle and I have great hopes for them. It is best I ignore them, for the moment, he thought. Later I'll remind them Miss Nagle demands respect at all times. I must admit I can't blame them for their amusement. What a lady she is!

Father Moylan, seething with frustration, knew Nano was correct. He was overstepping his authority because as parish priest, or anyone else for that matter, he had no right to forbid a person to build where they wished. But what really alarmed him was Nano's statement that she would build her convent elsewhere, when the needs in his own parish never diminished, and no one had ever done as much as Nano had. He knew, too, that hers was not an idle claim, because so many were always clamouring for her to work with them. He simply did not dare obstruct her in any way. A picture flashed through his mind of Nano at prayer. Yes, she did nothing without her God talk, and how often in the past she had accomplished the seemingly impossible, quietly, competently, and unobtrusively. Why should it be any different this time?

Swallowing his pride and mustering as much dignity as he could, he said, 'Miss Nagle, you are right, you are free to build where you wish. I ask only that you make sure that none of your works impinge on or endanger our Ursuline foundation, which is proving such a success. You know I have always supported you and will continue to do so. You have only to ask, as you have always been free to do, and I hope I can be of assistance.'

Nano, appreciative of his dignified response, did her best to reassure him. 'Father, thank you for your interest and support. As for the Ursuline Sisters, although they are growing more independent, I will always facilitate their development and maintain my interest in and association with them. You and I have worked together for many years, so you are familiar with how circumspect I am and how careful to avoid troubling the officials of the city. You can rest assured I will continue these practices.'

Satisfied with these assurances, Father Moylan hastened away, returning his focus to the many demanding calls he received daily. In March 1775 he hurried once more to Nano's cottage. After the usual pleasantries, he informed Nano of a new wave of proselytising which was sweeping the country.

'You and the Ursuline Sisters must continue your efforts to be careful,' he said. 'I have heard that the Incorporated Society for the Promotion of Charter Schools is beginning a new campaign to force Catholic children into their schools by a new law that they will now only accept Catholic children. This is a direct attack on you and your schools. You have no longer got your Uncle Joseph to defend you, your brothers are in Bath and our Bishop Butler's hands are tied – so do be most careful.'

'Every now and then we face a new challenge, don't we?' was Nano's reply. 'I don't think I fear as far as my schools are concerned. They are so popular and the Catholics become very angry at such laws, which they circumvent in every way possible. The merchants, the tradespeople and population in general see my schools as a boon because we have reduced the crime rate significantly through our education programmes. People feel much safer now. However, we can never be complacent, so thank you so much, Father. I'll certainly heed your warnings.'

In mid July Father Moylan was called to the Bishop's house to receive the news that he had been appointed Bishop of Kerry.

'I, together with all the people of your parish, will be sorry to see you go,' the Bishop told him. 'However, it is a great honour which you deserve. I know that the Ursuline Sisters will be sad to hear this news, and I am sure Miss Nagle will miss your wise counsel, as well.'

'Thank you, My Lord. I will miss all my friends here, too, but will do my best to serve the people of Kerry. I must go to see the Ursuline Sisters, and Miss Nagle and her group, to tell them the news before they hear it elsewhere.'

Although they were to feel keenly the loss of Father Moylan, Nano and the Ursuline Sisters rejoiced with him that his dedication and hard work were recognised by Rome. To them, Kerry seemed so far away. On his last visit to Nano, Father Moylan requested, 'Nano, I do have something to ask of you.'

Nano replied, 'If I can oblige, Father, I most certainly will. It is the least I can do to repay you for your years of support, interest and sound advice.'

'As each day passes I see you and your companions spend yourselves so unselfishly for the dispossessed and unwanted. Everywhere I look I see the results of your work, and become quite ashamed of my hasty action threatening to destroy your convent. The Bishop's confidence in you is also growing. I feel I am leaving you in supporting hands. Father Callanan is continuing his support, and being a religious he will be a huge help to you all. Now, I have a request. In a few years' time when I am settled as Bishop of Kerry, and your new congregation has hopefully grown, I would like you to make a foundation in Kerry.'

Nano looked surprised, but pleased. 'Father, I appreciate your confidence, and believe that, if it is God's will, we will prosper. I certainly accept your invitation to Kerry. Yes, as you say, the Bishop and Father Callanan continue to assist us, but we will miss your warm presence, and will keep you in our prayers.'

'I will be back from time to time,' Father Moylan assured her as he departed.

After Father Moylan's move to Kerry, Father Callanan became Nano's chief adviser on religious matters, especially as she searched for a religious rule for her congregation. She was particularly anxious that she and her companions would be able to officially begin their novitiate by Christmas 1775. This necessitated having a rule, even a provisional one.

After supper one Saturday evening in the autumn of 1775 when the sun's weak rays struggled to touch the roads of the better sections of the city with light – it had long given up the struggle to reach the lanes and alleyways – Nano and her two companions were discussing their future. Nano had returned from her hour of instructing the Ursuline boarders, a practice she had continued since the Ursulines had arrived.

'Mother Nagle, do you think Mary Anne will join us by Christmas?' Elizabeth asked, a frown of concentration on her face as she endeavoured to turn the toe of a sock she was knitting for the poor.

'I am sure she will,' Nano replied. She no longer attempted to knit anything but was, with Mary, preparing pictures as rewards for the children in the schools. 'I have been thinking we could officially begin our novitiate at Christmas when we expect Mary Anne. I think it would be a most appropriate time to begin our congregation. When you think about it, that's when God took human form in the person of Jesus, so that we could better form a relationship with him. I know some, including the Jansenists, say that God's purpose was to save us from our sins, but I prefer to think, like some theologians and our spiritual advisors, that God's main reason was to show us how to live and love as he does. I would like to think that the members of our congregation will be an example of God's love and mercy as Jesus was in his time. What do you think, would Christmas be a suitable time to begin?' Nano asked.

Both women embraced the idea with enthusiasm. When Nano approached Bishop Butler with this suggestion, he readily gave his permission.

'Have you heard from Miss Mulally recently, Mother Nagle?' Mary wanted to know one evening.

'No, I haven't,' Nano answered, then added regretfully 'But then, I haven't written for some time, either. We do send messages through Fathers Shortall and Callanan. I hear she is accomplishing great work, especially in her schools. I keep hoping that one day she will join us.'

Suddenly, the three were startled by a knock at the door. Nano opened it, expecting some poor person looking for assistance, but the man there, mud-spattered and weary, doffed his cap and handed her a letter. 'For you, Miss Nagle. I'm sorry miss,' he said before melting into the darkness. Nano took the letter inside, sat down and slit the letter open with her Nagle-crested letter opener, one of the few gifts she had retained from Uncle Joseph. Her companions noticed her face change. A white sadness took possession of it. They dared not ask about the letter's contents, but waited patiently for Nano to speak.

'It's about Mary, my sister,' Nano finally informed them. 'Dear Mary, she was always so quiet and timid. I knew she had been ill for some time, but Pierce, her husband, was hopeful she would recover. All her life she has been noted for her hospitality and warmth. Sadly, she died yesterday. She was only fifty-five. I think you might remember about five years ago I attended her daughter Sarah's wedding to William Creagh. I have only one sister, Elizabeth, left now.' Nano concluded sadly.

It was a sad evening for them all. The others encouraged Nano to share family memories of her sisters. It was the only way they could think of comforting her. 'Happy memories can be healing,' said little Elizabeth Burke sagely. It was while she was attending Mary's funeral that Nano heard the news that the American colonies had declared war on Britain in an effort to obtain their independence. Then, towards the end of the month, news arrived from Rome that Pope Pius VI had been elected. Nano wondered how both events would impact on Ireland and on her new foundation; in time, both would.

CHAPTER 11

On the morning of 24 December 1775 the sun rose tardily, as though reluctant to face the day. A playful breeze chased unresisting feathery white clouds across the grey sky as a small carriage drew up outside Nano's cottage. The three women within hastened to the door to welcome Mary Anne Collins. 'I haven't travelled far, you know,' Mary Anne laughingly responded when they welcomed her with morning tea.

'We are so happy to have you with us,' Nano said. A beaming Mary Fouhy and an equally happy Elizabeth Burke stood beside her. That afternoon the four gathered to reflect on the following day's ceremonies and festivities, for tomorrow they would begin officially their novitiate under the title of 'Sisters of Charitable Instruction of the Sacred Heart of Jesus'.

'Love must distinguish us. We must reflect the love of God to and for all,' Nano told them. 'Our love must be patient, enduring and non-selective. The loving heart of Jesus is our model.'

'Mother Nagle, you also are our model,' Mary Anne said.

The others nodded in agreement. Nano smiled, shook her head and said, 'We will need to think of our dress, as we don't want to wear a habit which would separate us from others, and of course it is forbidden by law. What should distinguish us is our manner of living, not what we wear. Have any of you thought about this dress?'

'Yes, since we came to live with you, Mother Nagle, Elizabeth and I have discussed this and have a few options,' Mary volunteered.

'Good,' Nano encouraged them, 'Would you like to share them?'

'We thought something black and plain, including a little bonnet, would perhaps be appropriate,' Mary answered.

'We must be thinking along the same lines, so I'll share my thoughts, too,' Nano said. 'I thought we could wear a simple black unadorned gown, and we could have a black silk handkerchief crossed over the front. Our cap could be a black plain one which would fit tightly. What do you think?' Nano asked.

'Yes, I like that idea,' Mary answered. Mary Anne and Elizabeth hastily agreed.

'We should think about our outside cloaks, too,' Mary Anne added. 'I notice your cough is often troublesome, Mother Nagle. We are frequently out and about the lanes, and of course going to and from school. Do you think we could have a long black woollen cloak, with a hood we can throw over our bonnets?'

'That is an excellent idea. I was thinking we would need some protection when out,' Nano agreed.

With that settled, Nano approached a dressmaker friend who soon provided them with their new dresses and cloaks. Their lives were poor, their meals frugal and they were often in want because ready money was not always available; but they had all come prepared for these discomforts. On 24 June 1777, the Feast of the Sacred Heart, Nano and her three companions made their first religious vows under the auspices of Bishop Butler, who affirmed Nano as the superior of the small group. They took simple vows of poverty, chastity and obedience, to be renewed annually.

Nano took advantage of the occasion to remind the Bishop of her goals. 'My Lord, I wish each member of my congregation to be a servant of the poor. I want them to be free of enclosure to be able to seek out the poor.'

'Mother Nagle,' the Bishop replied, 'I have heard it said that there is not a single garret in Cork which you do not know and do not visit. You obviously wish your sisters to do the same.'

'Yes, that is true, and I hope the religious names we have chosen reflect our vision.'

Nano had chosen the name Sister Saint John of God, Mary Anne became Sister Angela, Mary Fouhy Sister Joseph and Elizabeth Sister Augustine. It was many years before they could publicly use these names.

A couple of months later, Nano sat reflecting on what a beautiful day it had been. The children in the schools were progressing well under the guidance of optimistic teachers now that Nano's congregation had begun to materialise. The weather on this September evening seemed to be in tune with the happiness in Nano's small house.

'I must write to Teresa Mulally today. I feel I have been neglecting her of late and I have not told her about our lives here,' Nano told her companions.

'Do you think she will come to visit? We would love to have her. She might even join us!' Mary Anne spoke for them all.

'I will write to her,' Nano assured them. Later she sat at her desk to write to her old friend.

Dear Miss Mulally,
This is a pleasure I have been longing for, to tell you that I have invited three persons to join me in a congregation which will be devoted to the poor, and will ensure the continuation of my schools. What made me wait so long was that I could not get anyone to lead it and thought myself

too unworthy to do so. I know, however, that the Almighty makes use of the weakest means to bring about his work, so I decided to begin it myself. I am planning to send two sisters out to Bishop Moylan to make a foundation in Kerry, as he wished.

I am sending you a copy of the rule which we follow at present, and we have named ourselves 'Sisters of the Charitable Instruction of the Sacred Heart of Jesus'. Father Shortall, who will take this letter to you, will give you an account of us. My wish is that you will join us in this Society and I am sure that the great God will direct you to what is most to his glory.

Your affectionate friend,
Nano Nagle

As the year moved towards its end, Nano once more approached the foreman, this time with plans for her own convent.

'John,' she said, as she unfolded her instructions for the building, 'by now you have an idea of what I require in my buildings, and I am hoping the weather remains favourable so that you can finish it as soon as possible. As you are aware, we are quite cramped. I am hoping that other women will soon join us once they see this building completed.'

'Mother Nagle, it is always a pleasure to work for you. I must tell you that the latest bunch of apprentices from your schools is doing very well.'

After supper one evening, and when the sisters had walked around the silent building site where the trenches were ready for the walls, Nano told them that her brothers were also involved in building a new chapel in Bath. 'In Joseph's recent letter about their activities he told me that their wealth is growing, particularly David's, so that David was able to contribute £25 and he £10. They have both been appointed trustees. All the family seem to be happily settled in Bath. I am so pleased for them that they settled there, though I do miss them here,' Nano said.

When the foundations were laid and Nano could see the rising walls she once more wrote to Teresa Mulally, to whom she owed a letter.

Dear Miss Mulally,

Please accept my apologies for not answering your letter sooner. It gave me great pleasure to receive it and to hear that you and Miss Corballis were enjoying better health. You must be pleased that you both can now continue your great work and your success in all the good works you do.

It gave the sisters and me such joy to hear your favourable comments on the rule which I sent you. We ardently wish that you and your companions would join us. If that is not God's will, you can rely on us to assist you in establishing a house of our Society in Dublin, which you once requested.

I am building a house here, and when it is completed it will be fit for young ladies who have a dowry to join. We have had many trials of late but it would be too tedious to mention them. I think that with Divine assistance we will do well.

I am sending this letter with a friend of mine, Miss Creagh. She knows all the sisters and is good to the poor children. She has a great desire to meet you and your helpers. I know you will oblige her. My sisters and I continue our prayers for you.

Your affectionate friend,

Nano Nagle

As 1777 drew to a close, Nano and her sisters began to plan how they would celebrate Christmas, as well as planning the move to their new home, which they hoped would follow soon after. What they did not know was that it would not occur until over two years later.

'The number of beggars on the streets continues to trouble me, especially around Christmas time,' Nano said. 'We will move into a new house while so many have no home and no family. Christmas, too, reminds me of the Holy family searching for shelter and food for the night. I think of all the days and nights when they were escaping to Egypt and sought some-where to stay and something to eat. I was wondering if we could search out some homeless from the streets and invite them to Christmas dinner? We could have it in one of the completed rooms of the new house.'

For a moment the suggestion was met with silence. Through Elizabeth Burke's mind raced thoughts of where they would get the food and who would prepare it. Mary Anne wondered about how they would select the homeless from the great numbers that frequented the lanes and alleys, many of whom were dangerous. Mary wondered where they would obtain the money, which seemed of late to be very scarce. The thoughts vanished as quickly as they came. If Mother Nagle thought they could do it, that was sufficient. Mary Anne replied, 'I think that is a wonderful idea, Mother Nagle. I hesitated at first because I was thinking of the difficulties, but it is like you are always telling us: Divine Providence can provide, Divine Providence did provide and Divine Providence will provide. What is essential is that we respond in faith.'

The other two agreed, and for the next week or so they all set about preparing a Christmas Day meal for the fifty beggars they would invite. Nano's organisational skills came to the fore, so that there was little room for disaster on the day. When the dinner hour arrived Nano opened the door to her fifty beggars, some of whom she had difficulty in recognising. Somehow they had attempted to wash, and to trim their hair, after a fashion. Dressed in an assortment of comparatively clean, sometimes mismatched garments, they touched the sisters' hearts in their attempts to honour the occasion. When the shy, overawed visitors were seated, Nano officially welcomed them, thanked them for coming, said grace and served the first dish. She and the three sisters served their guests and conversed with them, gradually putting them at ease. When the day was drawing to a close each beggar received a little gift of leftovers; however, the largest gift had been the welcome they received, and the feeling of self-worth which was generated.

After the last guest departed, the four women, utterly exhausted, sat down. For a few minutes they were too weary to speak. Nano was the first to break the silence. 'Thank you so much to each of you for all your hard work, and above all for your loving hospitality. I'm sure you have provided our guests with a wonderful experience and happy memories.'

'I have gained so much from the experience, and I think I can speak for the others when I say we have been given more than we gave,' Mary Anne replied.

'That is certainly true,' the other two agreed.

Little Elizabeth began to laugh. The others looked at her enquiringly.

'I've never seen such fashions. I dare not wonder where some clothes came from.'

The others laughed. 'No, it's perhaps best not to know,' Mary Anne agreed, 'but wasn't it touching that they took such care with their appearance? I don't think I have ever seen Joe in different or clean clothes.'

'They were careful with their speech, too,' Mary commented. 'I've never heard old Charlie speak without using a few forbidden words. I wonder if they have been practising.' She smiled at the thought.

Nano stored all the comments in her mind, thinking that she would like to propose they make this an annual Christmas event. She wouldn't ask them now when they were all so tired. To her surprise Mary Anne asked, 'Do you think we could do this every Christmas Day?'

The idea was received with great enthusiasm, and thus began a tradition which lasted until the 1870s, when the Little Sisters of the Poor assumed this part of Nano's work.

The following year was a difficult one. The new building had eaten into Nano's available finances and she had unexpected problems with her schools. One evening Nano arrived home wet and tired. She was soon followed home by Mary Anne and Mary. Each was welcomed at the door by Elizabeth, who had been confined to home by a persistent cough – which did not prevent her from preparing a hot meal for them all. Each face brightened when, on opening the door, they were met by the aroma of a tasty Irish stew. After supper, Elizabeth remarked in a concerned voice, 'Mother Nagle you seem extra tired this week.'

'The last few weeks have not been happy ones, I am afraid,' Nano replied wearily. 'As you know, I can no longer visit every school every week, so I rely on my teachers to teach from their hearts. I have had to discharge all the mistresses, except for one whom I employed many years ago, as I could not bear to part with her. To my sorrow, I discovered that the mistresses I discharged had no interest in the care of the children. All they were interested in was the wage they earned. At first I could not believe it. How could this happen? It is against all my principles, which they well knew. My other problem, a lesser one, is my inability to access my money, which is tied up in bonds, mostly in France, who has now declared war on Britain. We are going to have to continue to live frugally, and to sometimes rely on the good will of others. I was hoping to found homes for elderly women, men and prostitutes and to make foundations in Dublin and Kerry, but all of that is out of the question until I don't know when.'

'After other women join us we will certainly be able to make these foundations, Mother Nagle,' Mary Anne consoled her.

'There is another matter I must raise with you,' Nano told them. 'We have been derided as "Walking Nuns", which is not pleasant. People think we should be confined behind walls. We must keep up our work in the schools and with the poor and abandoned, no matter what people call us. I have decided we would be wise never to dine out, but to confine our outings to our schools and our other works.'

Each of them agreed that was a wise move. 'To be truthful, I'm always too tired to be going out and about, anyway,' Elizabeth laughed.

'Now to a happier note: I am hoping to receive a copy of the rule of the Grey Sisters for us to study, to see if it is suitable for us to adapt. At the same time I hope for a parcel of the Office of Our Blessed Lady for us to pray. I believe it would be suited to our busy lives.'

Their recreation and discussion time did not last long that night, as the three sisters were aware of Nano's weariness, and of the heavy burdens she bore, which they felt powerless to lighten. A few days later their days were brightened by the arrival of Nano's nieces, her sister Elizabeth's daughters, who were on their way to visit their cousins in Cambrai, where they would also meet up with their parents. The inclement weather necessitated Nano spend a couple of days devoted to obtaining a passage to France for them. At last the weather permitted them to sail, and Nano sadly said farewell to her beloved nieces.

The next month Teresa Mulally made her long-awaited visit to Cork. She accompanied an ill friend, Mary, three girls whom she was chaperoning to the Ursuline boarding school, and an elderly lady. After delivering the girls to the Ursulines, then the elderly lady to her friends, Teresa and her friend went to their lodgings in Cove Lane. The next morning they went to visit Nano, who had just returned, dripping wet, through the falling rain. She had been to visit an elderly dying lady who had sent for her. Over a cup of tea and some of Elizabeth's oatcakes, Nano asked about their trip.

'Mother Nagle, what a trip! You have no idea how rough our roads are. We seemed to bounce from one hole to another, which the girls enjoyed, but it was not good for my poor bones. When we arrived at an inn on the way, soldiers were emerging, to the consternation of the old lady who shrieked in fright and threatened to swoon. This greatly amused the girls, which further angered the old lady. When we were coming through the Kilworth Mountains she clung to the seats of the coach, closed her eyes and continued to shriek about the possibility of highwaymen or invading French emerging from the mists. On our arrival at the next inn the poor keeper, in an effort to calm her, offered her a huge whiskey and a cake. The first she quaffed in one huge gulp; the other she ignored. The result was the blessing that she snored loudly for the rest of the trip! The girls were convulsed with laughter.'

Her listeners laughed at the vision. In the conversation which followed, Teresa, Nano and the sisters chatted about the various works in which they were engaged. Remembering Nano's promise of help, Teresa asked, 'Mother Nagle I'm wondering about the possibility of you now building and endowing a convent in Dublin.'

'I do wish I could,' Nano replied, 'but I'm very much in debt at present. The building of our convent has been a constant worry, and I also have staffing problems in my schools.'

Teresa looked so disappointed that Nano hastily added, 'Don't give up hope, Miss Mulally. Divine Providence will provide if we do our part, and you know we will do all we can to help.'

With this assurance Teresa looked more cheerful, for she knew that Nano always gave wise advice and always kept her promises.

'Have you found a satisfactory rule yet?' she asked.

'No I haven't. I thought it would be comparatively easy to procure copies of congregational rules, but how wrong I have been. I have tried to obtain copies from France. Of course they have to be brought here by trusted friends, as the establishment of convents is still forbidden. I have had the promise of some, but they have never been sent. I am expecting my sister Elizabeth French to obtain for me a printed copy of the rule and constitutions of the religious of the Third Order of Saint Francis, known as the Grey Sisters.'

'I haven't heard of them,' Teresa remarked.

Teresa stayed in Cork for about three weeks, spending as much time as she could with Nano and her community, as well as taking the opportunity to visit her old friend, Sister Angela Fitzsimons. When she left, she promised to return to see the progress of Nano's work. The evening after her departure, the four sisters, at their recreation hour, reminisced about the visit.

'It seems so quiet without her,' Elizabeth stated.

'I loved hearing about her schools, and kept thinking that many of her problems were similar to ours. She also had some amusing stories to tell,' Mary Anne reflected.

Nano said very little, but in her heart missed the company of her old friend. However, I must not be doleful, she thought as she looked around at her companions. I am very fortunate to have such devoted and dedicated women. Aloud she said, 'We will pray daily for Miss Mulally and continue to pray that God will send us more sisters.' It was sometimes difficult to be hopeful, especially when they looked next door to see the extensions to the flourishing Ursuline convent and schools.

Elizabeth, who had not been feeling well lately and was therefore more despondent than usual, remarked to Nano, 'Mother Nagle, I find it difficult to be positive when I see the number of professed sisters next door at the Ursuline Sisters. Every time I go out I see the extensions, and hear about the women who join them each year.'

Mary, who was busy making some bread, overheard, sighed, and agreed. 'Yes, it is difficult to be hopeful. The Ursulines have ten professed and expect to have twelve by 1780, I heard.'

'Yes, it can be difficult,' Nano agreed, 'I believe if it is God's will we will continue and flourish well beyond our dreams, so let us have hope and faith, and do our best in whatever we do – even making bread!' They all laughed, because bread-making was not Mary's forte.

To their delight, not long afterwards Nano was approached by two young women who wished to join them, and who came highly recommended. Nano accepted them and prudently watched their adaptation to religious life and their ability to live a community life. Miss Thompson immediately displayed a love of, and empathy with, the children. After a few weeks, however, Nano began to have doubts about their suitability. She spoke to Mary Anne. 'Mary Anne, in confidence, can you tell me how you think Miss Thompson and Miss Brady are progressing? You have spent more time with them than either Mary or Elizabeth.'

Mary Anne looked troubled. 'Mother Nagle I agree with you that Miss Thompson is a wonderful teacher. I find that she accepts advice and is willing to learn from others, but ...' She hesitated.

Nano smiled encouragingly, 'Religious life requires more, doesn't it? She is quite pleasant, but her heart is not committed to our way of life. Is that what you think, Mary Anne?'

'Exactly, Mother Nagle,' Mary Anne said with relief.

'I think we would all agree that Miss Brady does not belong here. Fortunately she has told me that she is leaving.'

By the end of the week both women had gone. Mary and Elizabeth breathed sighs of relief. 'Miss Brady was quite a trial,' Elizabeth whispered to Mary, who wholeheartedly agreed.

It wasn't long afterwards that Nano arrived home visibly upset. It was such an unusual sight that her concerned companions elicited a reason.

'I could not believe it! The Ursulines, who know that Miss Brady left us as an unsuitable candidate for religious life, have accepted her into their novitiate.'

'But they made an agreement with you that you would always be consulted on anyone whom they would accept,' Mary Anne exclaimed indignantly.

'Oh dear! I hope she won't cause too much friction. Of course, I agree you should have been consulted, Mother Nagle,' Elizabeth said softly.

'What are we going to do about it? This should not have happened.' Mary said.

'I think my next move will be to see the Bishop about it,' Nano answered.

With the encouragement of the others, Nano made an appointment with Bishop Butler. He had no hesitation in accepting Nano's views on Miss Brady, and had been present when Nano and the Ursulines had signed their agreement over the acceptance of candidates to the Ursuline congregation.

'Mother Nagle, thank you for informing me about this situation. You and I are both aware of how fragile the presence of convents is in Ireland. You and the Ursulines are providing a wonderful service to the city of Cork; and this service has no doubt encouraged the officials of the city to ignore your presence. You are to be commended for bringing these two institutions to our city. We must do all we can to preserve your mutual regard and support. Tomorrow you and I will visit the Ursulines to come to an agreement that neither community will accept a candidate who has been rejected by the other. I trust, Mother Nagle, this will be acceptable to you.'

Nano, well pleased with the outcome of her visit, went home to inform the others, and to ask their prayers for the following day's visit to the Ursulines.

Within a year of her last visit, Teresa arrived, this time with the news that she had a prospective candidate for Nano's congregation. 'Father Austin also commends her,' Teresa told Nano. 'I know you are always disappointed that neither Miss Corballis nor I feel called to join you, but we do our best to assist you by encouraging others to do so.'

The promised candidate, Miss Wolf, duly arrived from Dublin. It wasn't long, however, before it became apparent to Nano that, although Teresa and Father Austin had recommended her, she was not satisfactory. The three sisters agreed with Nano that she ask Miss Wolf to leave. Would they ever have suitable women join them? Would the life of their fragile community flicker out?

Nano's dismissal of Miss Wolfe met with criticism from many circles. She was a fine, talented young woman and her dismissal was an injustice, they claimed. 'Mother Nagle, can't you say something to justify your decision?' a concerned Mary Anne asked Nano, after a particularly scathing rumour reached them.

'Although I'm concerned that Miss Wolfe has applied to the Carmelites, I cannot in conscience tell my reasons, as perhaps it would tarnish her reputation. I am confident that all things will turn out for the best.'

Nano's views were vindicated when, within the month, Miss Wolf was refused entry by the Carmelites.

There was one bright note. Nano was delighted to receive the rule of the Third Order of Saint Francis, which she thought would be the answer to her search for a suitable rule. The other three waited in excited anticipation for Nano's opinion, as the uncertainty of a rule weighed heavily on their minds. Their hearts sank, as Nano's did, when she found that it too was unsatisfactory.

'No, this is not what I sent for,' Nano explained to them. 'It is not the rule of the Grey Sisters, although it is the rule of the Nursing Sisters from Nancy in France. I am hoping for a rule that accommodates both teaching and nursing. The latter is essential because of our work with the sick and the dying.'

'What did you think of their fasting laws?' Mary Anne asked. Nano had given each one a copy to read. Without hesitation, Nano replied, 'Their laws on strict fasting and abstinence certainly do not suit our purposes. Another aspect of the rule which I did not like was the amount of time dedicated to prayer. I wondered when they had time to do anything at all! You know I believe prayer, gospel reading and reflection are the foundation of our life, but we must build on this foundation with good works. We are called to be gospel people, to go out to serve. Our mission is one of service and I don't think that is the mission found in this rule. I'm afraid we must keep looking.'

It was an unsettling thought for them all: For how long would they have to continue the search? If they were to be recognised as a congregation, a rule was essential. To Nano, especially, it was like a dark cloud hovering above, but she was determined to accept only a rule which met her expectations. 'I know what I want,' Nano would inform the sisters, who smiled at this admission. How well they knew her determination. 'I think that the religious discipline practised in many European congregations does not suit Ireland. I believe firmly that there should be a balance between prayer and action. Both are essential, but for us there must be a balance. Another aspect is that priority must be given to the schools, for education is the great need at this time.'

'Well, as you are always telling us, Mother Nagle, Divine Providence will provide,' Mary Anne responded.

In moments when they tended to be despondent, she would say, 'Let us always remember that his Divine hand will always hold us.'

Nano received other rules, none of which suited their purpose. Father Moylan, always a practical helper, wrote to a friend of his, a Mère de Villaberneaux, the superior of the Sisters of Saint Thomas Villanova, whose work seemed similar to Nano's. In her reply she gave a summary of the rule, since it was not allowed that she send a copy. Nano read the rule with a lighter heart and gave it to the others for their opinion. One evening, after each of them had read, reflected, and prayed, they discussed it. Nano, pleased with it, not wishing to exert any influence, waited for each sister's judgement.

Mary Anne was the first to respond. 'What I particularly liked about it was the variety of works in which they are engaged – the orphans, the sick, schools, and care of the elderly – just as we are.'

'Don't forget the prisons and the prostitutes,' Mary said. 'Yes, I felt the rule suited us.'

'I also liked the fact that they worked with the old, and the impoverished men and women. I keep thinking of the joy of the beggars to whom we serve Christmas dinner, and how it transforms their lives,' Elizabeth added.

'I agree,' Nano said. 'Did you notice the broad scope of their educational programmes? I thought that they reflected our aims quite well. Like each of you, I am impressed that their multitude of works is similar to ours, and I liked also their emphasis on prayer and spiritual development. Aside from the fact that they take perpetual vows I find the rule very attractive, so I am pleased that you do too. However, we will need to reflect on it more, and pray before we reach a decision.'

'Do you think trouble is brewing again, Mother Nagle?' Mary Anne asked one evening. 'My brother thinks that Lord George Gordon in England will stir up anti-Catholic feeling which could spread to our country.'

'I wouldn't be surprised,' Nano replied. 'When Sir George Saville introduced the Catholic Relief Act last year, I thought there would be a backlash of anti-Catholic feeling. We must continue to be vigilant. Of course the Act won't affect many people and was only passed because Britain needs to build up its army to fight the American colonies, France and Spain, so needs more soldiers. Catholics can now join the army because the Act absolves them from taking the religious oath.'

When she went as usual to the Ursuline convent to instruct the boarders in their religious knowledge, one Sunday evening the 11 December, Nano was horrified to find the Ursuline who answered the door was dressed in her religious habit. Nano demanded to see them all. 'Sisters why have you suddenly decided to wear your religious dress when we fear anti-Catholicism is rearing its head? You jeopardise our existence here where, with a great effort, we have established such a positive atmosphere. After eleven years, there is absolutely no need for you to dress as you have.'

'Mother Nagle, we believe you are too timid about this. Nothing will happen. Anyway, it is such a cold winter and we are much warmer in our habits. It would be dangerous to our health to remove them now for secular dress,' Mother Augustine Coppinger claimed.

Nano shook her head in frustration and curtly replied, 'Father Moylan will be in town soon and, when he sees you have dressed in habits, the air will be warm enough for you to change.'

On his arrival, Father Moylan recommended that the nuns reflect seriously on their course of action. 'Is it worth risking your safety for the consolation of wearing religious dress?' he asked. The sisters argued and pleaded, until eventually he agreed that they continue to do so, but warned that they risked persecution.

The winter proved difficult for Nano and her sisters as they struggled for warmth in their small cottage. Both Nano and Elizabeth were troubled by constant coughs. 'I wish we could convince Mother Nagle to take more care of herself. I have suggested that she give up her strict fasting on Wednesdays and Fridays, but to no avail. The answer is always the same. She claims that she so wasted her early life and was so selfish that she feels this is one way of making amends,' Mary Anne confided to Mary.

'Well, she certainly never thinks of herself now,' Mary replied. 'Yet she insists that we do not perform such strict penances. Look at the way she discards some rules because of their penitential demands. By the way, did you ever hear anything like her cure for sore eyes?'

Mary Anne laughed. 'You mean that time when an icy wind seemed to pierce every bone, and, although she had very sore eyes, she insisted on going to the North Gate School, then claimed her eyes were much better after the experience. They did improve, too, and Mother Nagle claimed that God always gives the strength necessary to do His work.' Mary Anne continued, 'I'm really looking forward to moving into our new building. It will be so much better for Mother Nagle and Elizabeth's health, which do worry me.'

'Yes, I agree. It's over two years since the builders began. Of course, if Mother Nagle had thought only of herself, we would have been in long ago. I had mixed feelings when Mother Nagle told the Ursulines she would tell the builders to pull down a part of our brick wall, so that cargoes of stone could be taken through for their extensions; however, if she hadn't, it would have cost the Ursulines a great deal of money, so I really could not begrudge Mother's generosity.'

In June 1780, there was great rejoicing when at last they could occupy their new convent. As usual though, things did not run smoothly. The sisters were used to Nano's oft-repeated saying 'the greatest works meet with the greatest difficulties', which was her response on this occasion. They had been busily packing their few possessions when they heard of what became known as 'the Gordon Riots'. It was difficult not to hear about them because of the fear which they engendered in the Catholic community.

The sisters discussed the bad news. They couldn't help wondering if, or when, they would be affected. Mary Anne, returning late from a call to the tenements near the North Gate, where a summer fever was prevalent, joined the conversation when Nano was telling them: 'Lord George Gordon set up a Protestant Association in protest against the Catholic Relief Act. They are an anti-Catholic group who have gathered a petition to appeal against the Act. I have heard that they have aroused such antagonism that 60,000 have signed the petition.'

'My father told me that other troublemakers are using the occasion to make life difficult for Catholics and their supporters, and that riots have broken out all over London,' Elizabeth added.

'Yes, my brother told me that today. He said that rioters have attacked and burnt the houses of the leaders of the Catholic Relief Act, like those of the Marquis of Bockingham, the Duke of Devonshire, Lord Mansfield and George Saville. They have also looted and burnt churches, presbyteries and houses of leading Catholics,' Mary Anne said.

'I heard that too, but the Act doesn't affect many Catholics, does it?' Mary contributed. 'I believe the militia were slow to act during the riots so things got out of control.'

'That's true,' Nano said. 'George III insisted the troops be called, and finally the riots ended, but the anti-Catholic feeling is rife. I think we will have to be extra careful about our move to the convent, which I would like to occur on 15 July so that we can celebrate the Feast of Our Lady of Mount Carmel there on the following day.' They all agreed that it was a wonderful idea, especially as they were almost ready for the move.

'First thing in the morning, you and I, Mary Anne, will go to ask some of our friends if they will help us move our beds and anything else heavy, before the sun rises on the morning of the 15th and there are people about. I know that our street people will be around, but we are quite safe with them. Will you be able to come with me if you are not called out again, or if you don't have another commitment?'

'I'll be happy to come with you, Mother Nagle.'

On the morning of the move they were all up at about three o'clock. Mary Anne and Elizabeth went to the new convent to receive anything which arrived. Nano, Mary and their friends stole into the darkness of the night, carrying their goods 'like thieves', as Nano said afterwards. Nano had warned the Ursulines to be careful to say nothing about the move, and, of course, she and her companions had remained silent about it.

On 9 September 1780, the night of the nativity of the Blessed Virgin Mary, the first elections took place. Mother Nagle was re-elected superioress by a secret vote and was confirmed in her office by the Jesuit priest, Nicholas Barron, who had been appointed superior, as was the practice at that time.

During the following year, the American War of Independence continued to occupy the British Government's attention. When the British surrendered at Yorktown on 4 December 1781, they had no other option than to give concessions to Catholics by granting to them a series of relief acts. According to these acts, the Catholic Church was legally recognised, and Catholic teachers were free to teach, but not endow schools. That meant that for at least thirty years Nano had been acting outside the law, and indeed was still doing so by running and supporting her school system.

There was a ray of hope for Nano and the sisters when, in April 1782, a Miss Oliffe entered and began her novitiate. To Nano's delight, it seemed that at last, after seven years, they had found a suitable candidate. After Miss Oliffe's reception on 21 November 1782, the Feast of the Presentation of the Blessed Virgin Mary, Nano expressed her relief to Mary Anne: 'I have never met anyone in Ireland who has such zeal, spirit of mortification and humility. How happy she is when helping others – which I think she would be willing to do from morning until night.'

Miss Oliffe's entry was soon followed by that of the eighteen-year-old Miss Hodnett. From the age of twelve, Miss Hodnett had expressed a desire to enter Nano's congregation. Her family was well known to Nano, who welcomed this well-educated, talented and commonsensical young woman, who she believed would be a 'bright ornament' to the congregation. In the same year, 1783, Miss Connell, a relative of Nano's, and Anto Tobin entered the novitiate. There were now six women living in the new convent. Nano spent many hours and a great deal of money on the education and spiritual formation of her novices. But it was the living witness of Nano and the sisters which was the most powerful influence. All were formed in and by love, the love of God, as symbolised by the Sacred Heart, the enduring and ever-present love of God for all creation. Nano modelled this love in the ordinary every day, and expected her sisters to do the same. She had been a country child who first met God in her country family and in their farm life. She wished her sisters to live as a loving family and, in the midst of the city, brought a touch of the country by building a garden at the back of the convent where the sisters could walk in safety, breathe fresh garden air and find God in the quiet and beauty of His creation.

Nano's happiness on the entry of the young women was overshadowed by her worry over Elizabeth's growing fragility. 'The doctors don't seem to be able to do anything for her,' Nano said to Mary Anne, who frowned.

'Unfortunately, no. We are all concerned about her, Mother Nagle. She has struggled for so long to help wherever she can, but now everything is beyond her. All, including our novices, have shown great care for her. They are so impressed by her patience and good humour.'

Nano looked out the window to where Elizabeth, wrapped in a blanket, sat enjoying the afternoon sun. Mother Nagle looks so sad, Mary Anne thought, as Nano softly said, 'I too admire her cheerful acceptance of her illness; it must be a great burden for her.' Distressed, Nano was overtaken by a severe bout of coughing.

'We are concerned about you too, Mother Nagle,' Mary Anne said.

'I'll grow so old you'll all be tired of me!' Nano laughingly responded. 'Now for good news: we have had a remarkable response to my appeal for funds to help build my home for elderly women. I am going to see John tomorrow about it. I'll tell the other sisters tonight.'

'Mother, we will all rejoice with you, especially Elizabeth who, in particular, has loved working with the elderly destitute.'

Nano said sadly, 'I am afraid she won't be here for the opening, but at least she'll have the happiness that my dream is about to be realised.'

As Nano had predicted, the building was not quite ready when, after the entry of Miss Tobin, they gathered around the dying Elizabeth Burke. As the watery April sun sank, Elizabeth rose to eternal life. Silent tears crept down Nano's face. Mary Anne and Mary struggled unsuccessfully to contain theirs, while the novices' moist eyes displayed their love for the kind, gentle little Elizabeth whom they had known for such a short time. A few days later, they and many friends attended Elizabeth's burial in Saint John's, the cemetery for the poor. That evening a saddened community reflected on Elizabeth's life and burial.

'Who were those ragged people standing outside the cemetery gate?' Miss Connell asked.

Nano looked at her and smiled. 'Elizabeth would have been surprised to see them there. They were some of the beggars who have been to our Christmas dinners.'

'You wouldn't believe it,' Mary said, 'but I'm sure I saw Joe and Old Charlie. They looked much older, but had made an effort to dress up.'

'Yes, I saw them too,' Mary Anne said.

'I can imagine Elizabeth laughing and saying, "I wonder where they got those clothes"' Nano reminisced. 'That reminds me: we'll soon be opening the home for the elderly women, and I think we need some regulations, so it might be a good idea for us to work on them. One thing I would insist on is that the women we accept be of sober habits.'

'Definitely. We've all seen what overindulgence in drink has done to people and families,' Mary Anne spoke for them all.

It wasn't long before they had formulated a series of regulations which would assist the elderly to live in safety, comfort and happiness, as well as assure them of spiritual development and consolation. 'We must make sure that no one dies alone, and that each one is buried with dignity and love,' Nano told them. 'I'll make sure of the latter by buying plots for their burial,' she added.

'Mother Nagle, we know you have been buying plots and burying the destitute for many years,' Mary Anne smiled.

'It pained me to see the way they were bundled into carts and buried without ceremony, and with no one to care about them, so I have been buying plots in Saint John's,' Nano admitted.

Over the next few weeks, Mary Anne and Mary became increasingly concerned about Nano's failing health. 'She seems to have aged since Elizabeth's death, and her cough has worsened, don't you think?' Mary asked one day.

'I agree with you, Mary. I do wish she would desist from her fasting, or at least have some rest from the schools, or her work in the tenements. We've tried unsuccessfully for years though, so I suppose we won't succeed now.'

Their conversation was interrupted by a knock at the door, which Mary Anne answered. Standing there were a well-dressed young man, and an equally expensively dressed woman, obviously his mother, who requested to see Nano. Mary Anne, in her usual gracious manner, welcomed them and fetched Nano. After some time the three emerged, the visitors obviously well pleased with the visit. After their departure, Nano described their purpose to her curious companions. 'My visitors', she explained, 'were Mrs Dove and her son, Edmond, who are moving to Lisbon. They had a huge problem.'

Nano's companions looked interested and a little puzzled, but waited patiently for Nano to continue.

'Mrs Dove has a simple daughter who would find the move too traumatic. She is unable to cope with anything new or different, so Edmond suggested to his mother that they appeal to us for help. They asked that we look after her here in the convent where we could keep her safe. They offered £300 for her support. I had many arguments against our acceptance of this responsibility.'

'I think you took the right decision to refuse, even though we badly need the £300,' Mary Anne said.

'Yes,' Mary agreed, 'I know we aren't enclosed, but we do not have the facilities to cope with Miss Dove.'

'Oh, but I did accept her,' Nano said softly. 'I just could not bear to see their pain and anxiety, or the confusion of their daughter, and I know God always provides.'

There was silence. Finally Mary Anne said, 'Well of course we will support your decision, Mother Nagle, and do all we can to care for Miss Dove.' Mary agreed.

The Doves happily set sail for Lisbon and Miss Dove came to live at the convent, but daily became more incapacitated. Although docile and easily managed, she required constant care, which the sisters endeavoured to give. After a particularly exhausting day, Mary confided in Mary Anne. 'I'm not complaining or criticising Mother Nagle, and Miss Dove is a sweet person, but I do think that in this case her heart ruled her head.'

Mary Anne gently responded, 'When we write our rule perhaps we should add that we never undertake such a responsibility again.' With this observation the conversation ended, but the experience did have an impact on their future rule.

CHAPTER 12

It was a great joy to all, especially the ailing Nano, when, on 4 November 1783, Miss Oliffe was professed. However, just one year later, just after Nano's death, she was stricken with tuberculosis and allowed to go to her parent's house, where she died in 1803. Nano also had the happiness of seeing the reception of Miss Hodnett, now Sister Agnes. She too fell ill, and died shortly after her profession in June 1785.

As her strength failed, Nano increasingly struggled to attend her schools and minister to the sick. Mary Anne and Mary witnessed this struggle each morning as, after her hour's prayer and Mass at Saint Finbarr's, Nano set off leaning on her stick, through fog, rain or the occasional sunshine. Fortunately, they were unaware of the ulcers on her feet, or the state of her knees from the hours she spent in prayer. These were revealed only after her death. They were aware, however, of her persistent and hacking cough, and were not surprised when she announced that she was writing her will.

'I have obligations to my family,' Nano informed Mary Anne and Mary, 'but I will leave sufficient for you to maintain at least five sisters. Of course, my brothers will never see you in want. Mary Anne, when I die it will be your responsibility to look after the foundation.'

Mary Anne was too overcome to answer. 'You'll be with us a long time yet, Mother Nagle!' Mary managed to exclaim, but even she did not believe this.

As Lent progressed, Nano's regime of fasting, prayer and penance continued into Holy Week. As usual, she spent her time in the schools, reading the gospel story of the Passion to the different groups of children.

'Mother Nagle, would you like one of us to do some of the reading?' Mary Anne asked.

'It gives me strength to do so,' was Nano's reply. 'I see their faces, intent with empathy for the suffering Jesus. They know what it feels like to be rejected and to suffer.'

Holy Thursday arrived, and when the vigil commenced Nano knelt before the Blessed Sacrament. She seemed to lose all account of time. When Mary found her still there some hours later, undecided what to do, she went to Mary Anne. 'I'm worried about Mother Nagle. She is so ill; she should be in bed resting.'

'Mary, don't worry. She is so deep in God's presence she doesn't feel the pain. She'll go to bed when she is ready.'

Somewhat consoled, Mary went to bed, not realising that it would be eleven hours before Nano would do so.

Easter was a joyous festival for them all. Nano appeared to have revived after her hours of prayer and fasting. As she usually did on special occasions, Eleanor Fitzsimons sent some delicacies for their enjoyment. Over the months, Eleanor had expressed concern about Nano's health and, endeavouring to help, had often sent specials for Nano's diet. After Easter week, Nano returned to her school rounds and her visits to the lanes, although she often struggled to do so. 'I take such delight in it,' she would protest when someone suggested that she stay at home. One Wednesday Nano looked particularly ill. 'Mother Nagle, wouldn't you consider resting today?' Mary Anne asked.

'I promised little Des Kelly I'd visit his granny who, as you know, is quite ill and is blind. She so looks forward to my visits, and I couldn't break a promise to poor little Des, whose life is so difficult,' Nano answered.

Mary Anne smiled resignedly. 'Perhaps you could break your walk by calling into your friend, Margaret Creagh.'

'Yes, I'll do that,' Nano assured Mary Anne.

When Nano reached the Creaghs she found she certainly needed to rest, as she could not go a step further. Margaret Creagh kept looking anxiously at her friend, who at one stage had a fit of coughing, followed by a haemorrhage.

'You can't go any further,' Margaret protested. 'I'll order a carriage to take you home where you must go to bed.'

'I truly feel much better after this rest here,' Nano assured her. 'There is no need for a carriage. I'll walk, but will rest when I reach home.'

Nano set off and, after many stops to regain her breath, she eventually reached home. After about an hour's rest she decided she could do a few little things before the others arrived from their various ministries. Although none of them spoke to Nano about her obvious weakness, they murmured amongst themselves. When she suffered a spell of dizziness Mary Anne grasped the opportunity.

'Mother Nagle, it's off to bed with you. Mary and I will help you upstairs and get you into bed, and then I'll send for the doctor.'

'Do you think she is dying?' a frightened Miss Oliffe whispered to Miss Hodnett.

'I think she is. What are we going to do without her?' an equally dismayed Miss Hodnett answered. Neither were scared by death, with which they were all too familiar, but by the thought of life without their Mother Nagle.

When the two returned from upstairs, they explained that Nano was certainly very ill, but had forbidden them to send for the doctor. The next morning her condition had not improved. Eleanor Fitzsimons, who hadn't seen Nano since she struggled home the previous afternoon, accosted Mary, from whom she heard the news of Nano's condition and her refusal to let them call the doctor.

'I'm sending for the doctor,' Eleanor said firmly.

The alarmed doctor ordered blistering and bleeding, as was the practice of the time. These increased Nano's suffering, but not a word of complaint passed her lips. The grieving sisters gave her all the loving care they could. A smile lit up her face each time someone came to sit beside her to pray. There was often a message or a little gift that she wished given to one of her beloved poor.

'Mary, would you take that little knick-knack on the shelf to Johnnie Lane? He has improved so much.'

'Mary Anne, would you and Miss Hodnett visit the poor little Pratt family? It would be a good idea if you took some food, and a little of that medicine for their sick baby. Perhaps someone could take some blankets to the Kelly family ...' and so on.

On 25 April, when her confessor, Father Callanan, arrived, Nano asked if he would anoint her. He promised he would do so the next morning. 'Is there anything else I can do for you, Mother Nagle?' he asked.

'Only one thing, Father: please take care of my schools.'

'Indeed I will,' he promised.

The news of Nano's impending death spread rapidly along the canals and lanes, through the tenements and beyond the prison walls. Hardened hearts melted in sorrow. Nano's schools closed, the children and teachers too heartbroken to attend. Many wept, and even the most unkempt crept into the churches to pray, or merely sit, not knowing what to do.

In Nano's room, the sisters knelt around her bed. Mary Anne, who longed to hear her voice once more, said, 'Do you have a last message for us, Mother?'

In the silence that followed they all thought that a word would not be given. Her life had been her word, they reflected; yet they wished to hear the beloved voice just once more.

With an effort, Nano opened her dark eyes, still impressive although devoid of their former spark. She seemed to look at each one with love. In a surprisingly strong voice she said, 'Love one another as you have done until now.' She paused, then added, 'Spend yourselves for the poor.'

She didn't speak again, but they knew she was aware of their presence and their prayer. Shortly after midday Nano opened her eyes and smiled at them, closed her eyes again and, with a sigh, quietly entered into the loving arms of her God.

It was difficult to grasp the fact that she was no longer with them. Mary Anne, as Nano had wished, led the sorrowing group through their preparations for Nano's funeral. The Ursuline Sisters next door mourned the death of Nano as their 'holy and venerated foundress'. Before the day was over, they celebrated a Solemn Office and a High Mass in their chapel, as they had promised to do years ago on the foundation of their house. Earlier, when the Ursulines had heard that Nano intended to be buried in Saint John's cemetery, they objected strongly. Eleanor was particularly distressed. 'Mother Nagle, you are our foundress and should be buried in our cemetery between our two houses.' Nano eventually capitulated, on the condition that all of her sisters be buried there.

The sun shone weakly as the sisters gathered to bury the body of their beloved Mother Nagle near the boundary wall of the two convents. As the last shovel of earth was raised, the birds twittered excitedly in the trees above, and for a few minutes the soft rays of the sun grew stronger as they reached the grave. Five lonely women silently walked away to a home which seemed empty without their Mother Nano.

In the following years, they often wondered if Nano's dreams would become realities. Three days after Sister Anto Tobin pronounced her vows on 3 January 1785, Sister Joseph Connell died from the same disease as her relative, Mother Nagle. Both Nano and Mary Anne had believed her to be a treasure for the congregation, and Mary Anne felt her loss deeply. The sisters' hopes were dashed again a few days after Sister Joseph's death, when the recently professed Sister Anto Tobin left the congregation to join the Ursulines because she believed there was no future for Nano's congregation. Her sister, Mary Tobin, had left a few weeks after entering. Once again the congregation teetered on the brink of extinction. For years, Mary Anne heroically led the little community through what appeared to many as the death knell of the congregation, but – imbued with Nano's spirit – her courage and faith never wavered. Perhaps one of the greatest threats to their future occurred when Bishop Butler, in late 1786, suddenly left the priesthood to resume the title of Lord Dunboyne. Even this apostasy of Bishop Butler, under whose protection the congregation existed, did not deter Mary Anne. It was a great relief when Father Moylan, Nano's old friend, was appointed Bishop of Cork.

Over the years of extreme poverty, illness, death, search for a suitable rule and ecclesiastical uncertainty, Mary Anne steadfastly led the struggling congregation. When Mary Anne died in 1804 she was the only one of Nano's companions still living, but she saw what Nano had long dreamed for: foundations in Killarney, Co. Kerry (1793), Dublin (1794), Waterford (1798), North Presentation, Co. Cork (1799) and Kilkenny (1800). Growth was slow, but gradually Nano's dream of being of service to anyone who needed it has taken her congregation across the world, to wherever the poor are found and wherever injustices exist.

BIBLIOGRAPHY

Books:

Annals, South Presentation Convent Cork, trans. Sister Mary Magdalen de Pazzi Leahy.

Annals, Presentation Convent, Bandon.

Clarke, Sister Ursula, *The Ursulines in Cork Since 1771*, Ursuline Convent, Blackrock, Cork, 2007.

Congregation for the Causes of the Saints, Prot.N.1494, *Cause of beatification and canonisation of the servant of God Nano Nagle (1718–1784), foundress of the Sisters of Charitable Instruction of the Sacred Heart of Jesus, afterwards Sisters of the Presentation of the Blessed Virgin Mary: Positio Super virtutibus*, i–iii, Congregation of the Causes of Saints, Rome, 1994.

Consedine, M. Raphael, *Listening Journey: A Study of the Spirit and Ideals of Nano Nagle and the Presentation Sisters*, Congregation of the Presentation of the Blessed Virgin Mary, Vic., 1983.

Defoe, Daniel, 'The Education of Women', *English Essays from Sir Philip Sidney to Macaulay: Addison, Steele, Swift, Defoe, Johnson and others*, ed. Charles W. Eliot, P. F. Collier and Son Company, New York, 1910.

Durant, Will and Ariel, *The Age of Voltaire: A History of Civilization in Western Europe from 1715 to 1756, with Special Emphasis on the Conflict Between Religion and Philosophy*, Simon and Schuster, New York, 1965.

Hutch, W., *Nano Nagle: Her Life, Her Labours and their Fruits*, McGlashen & Gill, Dublin, 1895.

Leahy, Maurice, *The Flower of Her Kindred: A Biographical Study of Nano Nagle of Ireland, foundress, pioneer of popular education and noted leader in Sociology in the eighteenth century*, The Eldridge Company, Michigan, 1944.

Martin, M. Marie de Saint Jean, *The Spirit of Saint Angela*, Imprimatur, New Jersey, 1950.

Moran, Patrick Francis, *Historical Sketch of the persecutions suffered by the Catholics of Ireland*, M.H. Gill, Dublin, 1884.

O'Connell, Mrs Morgan John, *Nano Nagle: A Woman's Record of a Woman and Her Work*, serialised in *The Irish Catholic*, September–December 1889, reprinted by Australian Presentation Society, Australia, 1998.

O'Farrell, Sister Pius, *Nano Nagle: Woman of the Gospel*, Cork Publishing Limited, Cork, 1996.

O'Farrell, Sister Pius, *Breaking of Morn, Nano Nagle (1718–1784) & Francis Moylan (1735–1815): a Book of Documents*, Cork Publishing Limited, Cork, 2001.

O'Mahony, Colman, *In the Shadows: Life in Cork, 1750–1930*, Tower Books, Cork, 1977.

Savage, Roland Burke, *A Valiant Dublin Woman: The Story of Georges Hill (1766–1940)*, M.H. Gill and Son Ltd, Dublin, 1940.

Smith, Charles, *The Ancient and Present State of The County and City of Cork, Containing a natural, civil, ecclesiastical, historical, and topographical description thereof*, Vol. I, John Connor, Cork, 1815.

Young, Arthur, *A Tour in Ireland: with general observations on the present state of that kingdom, made in the years 1776, 1777 and 1778, and brought down to the end of 1779*, Vol. II, J. Williams (printer), Bonham, Dublin, 1780.

Walsh, T.J., *Nano Nagle and the Presentation Sisters*, Dublin, 1959.

Waters, Peter M., *The Ursuline Achievement: a philosophy of education for women: Saint Angela Merici, the Ursulines and Catholic education*, Colonna, North Carlton, Victoria, 1994.

Articles:

Fleming, David, 'Public Attitudes to Prostitution in Eighteenth-Century Ireland, Irish Economic and Social History Society of Ireland,' *Irish Economic and Social History*, Dublin, 2005, no. 32, pp. 1–18.

Kelly, James, 'A Most Inhuman and Barbarous Piece of Villainy: An Exploration of the Crime of Rape in Eighteenth-Century Ireland', *Eighteenth-Century Ireland Society*, Ireland, 1995, no. 10, pp. 78–107.

Kelly, Sister Sheila, 'Never Too Late: The Twenty Ladies of Saint Finbarr's Cemetery', *Outlines*, Presentation Sisters, South West Province, Cork, Summer, 2001.

McCann, Peadar, 'Cork City's Eighteenth-Century Charity Schools', *Journal of Cork Historical and Archaeological Society*, Ireland, 1979, no. 84, pp. 105–6.

Raughter, Rosemary, 'A Discreet Benevolence: female philanthropy and the Catholic resurgence in eighteenth-century Ireland', *Women's History Review*, Taylor and Francis Group, Oxford, UK, 1997, 6:4, pp. 465–87.

Robinson, Valerie, 'Barbados's memorial to Irish slaves reignites Cromwell Row', *Irish News*, 4 May 2009.

Websites:

Laws in Ireland for the Suppression of Popery: Commonly known as the Penal Laws, comp. M. Patricia Schaffer, University of Minnesota Law Library On-Line, 2000.
<http://library.law.umn.edu/irishlaw/intro.html>

McCarthy, Kieran, *Cork Through My Eyes: Challenges and Reclamation, Cork, c.1690–c.1750, Cork Heritage: A Blog about Cork City, Heritage and Photography*, History Articles, Historical Walking Tours.
<http://corkheritage.ie>

'Obituary: with anecdotes of Remarkable Persons.' *Gentleman's Magazine and Historical Chronicles*, Nicholson, Son and Bentley, London, 83:1, p. 236.
<http://books.goggle.com.au./books>

O'Connor, Basil, *Nagles of Ballygriffin: County Cork. Nangle, Costello, Nagle: A comprehensive study of the origin and early history of the Nangle, Costello and Nagle families and their environment*, pp. 93–8.
<http://www.naglemedieval.com>

O'Donnell, Ian, 'Sex Crime in Ireland, Extent and Trends', *Judicial Studies Institute Journal*, Judicial Studies Institute, Dublin, 2003, 3:1, pp. 91–2. <http://www.jsijournal.ie>

Rousseau, Jean Jacques, 'On the Education and Duties of Women'. Quoted in Men's Voices on Women – 18th Century, Women's History. About.com, part of New York Times Company. <http//womenshistory.about.com>

'Through Corridors of Life: A look at Nano Nagle's influence on Educational Psychology in Ireland,' *The Irish Psychologist: Bulletin of the Psychological Society of Ireland*, Dublin, March 1976, 2:8.
<http://www.presentationsistersunion.org/_uploads/rsfil/01079.pdf>

Rosa P E Security. 1e